ECSTASY

URBAN READS BOOKSTORE
3008 Greenmount Ave. Balto, MD 21218
oururbanreads.com
443.552.1094

By

Donald Reynolds & M.I. Waldo

Published By

Uncaged Minds Publishing

P.O. Box 436

Green Bay, Wisconsin 54305

uncagedmindspublishing@gmail.com

uncagedmindspublishing.com

Printed in the United States of America.

PUBLISHER'S NOTE:

ACKNOWLEDGMENTS

M.I. Waldo and Donald Reynolds proudly dedicate this literary work to the loyal readers and new readers of street fiction, as well as our fellow authors who also expose their life experiences shamelessly. Because it's all about contributing to the elevation of our social and economic conditions by way of holding up a mirror, reflecting our every day realities.

As our urban culture continues to evolve and expand and becomes more inclusive than ever, characters of all nationalities will naturally appear. This book is dedicated to all those who are brave and curious enough to venture into our dark world by way of words, sentences and paragraphs. Welcome to the ghetto.

To those in prison, and also those trapped in the agony of prison-like conditions in the streets this book belongs to you.

Chapter 1

As rays of early morning sunlight began cascading through the narrow slits of her very expensive vertical blinds, Alexis was awakened by the buzzing noise coming from her digital alarm clock sitting on the nightstand beside her bed.

Once again she had fallen asleep still dressed in her work clothes. She managed to wrestle out from beneath a thick red and green Gucci comforter to put an end to the annoying chime, then she unclasped her Rolex with the diamond and white-gold bezel and set it on the nightstand next to a small framed photograph of her daughter.

After she removed her midnight-blue business suit and her pink lace panties, Alexis just sat there on the edge of her bed massaging her throbbing left arm, still completely drained from the previous night's work. Her arm had been bothering her for several weeks now, but when her cell phone began ringing she was able to block out the tingling sensation she felt. And before answering the call, she quickly opened the drawer in her nightstand and pulled out a tan-colored 7-inch silicone vibrating dildo, then she crawled back into bed with it in her hand and answered the phone. She immediately heard the familiar recording that she'd been expecting: "You have a prepaid call from an inmate at a federal correctional facility. Press '5' to accept the call or press '7' to block any calls of this nature —"

BEEP! She pressed '5' and a man's voice came bemoaning through the phone's headset. Then she wiped at her stunning almond-shaped brown eyes and grinned. Of course, she knew it was her husband-to-be, Stephon.

"Sorry I'm late, ma. They just opening up my cage for the day. You been waiting for papi?"

Before she answered, Alexis removed her silk and lace bra. "Yes, but waiting for you, papi's, taking its toll on my health," she replied in a whisper. "I'm trying my best to be strong, but—"

Stephon cut in. "Don't talk like that! C'mon, mami, it's hard enough on me dealing with the shit I'm going through in this bitch...stressin' and shit. At leas' you're free, Lex. Now, you collect that twenty racks yesterday, right?"

"I'm sorry...yes, I collected it."

"Good, go blow five of that on something pretty for yourself. I'll let you know later where to Western Union the rest. Understand me?"

"Yes, and thank you."

"Papi takes good care of you, right? So, you just need to stay strong for us. Now look, ma. You know what time it is, open your legs...let's play for a few minutes."

Without responding, Alexis parted her butter pecan-colored thighs, then began sucking on the head of the toy while gently caressing and running circles around her light-brown stiffened nipples. In her mind she visualizes her fiancé her on top of her.

2

Her entire body trembled as she seductively moaned into the phone before guiding the vibrating toy between her inner thighs while Stephon's deep controlling voice led her along.

Alexis enjoyed his slight Spanish accent, and inhaled then arched her back at the same time the head of the toy reached her clit. This aroused her and allowed her thoughts and imagination to carry her back to a time and place before her lavish lifestyle came tumbling down on her, before her arrest and prison bit. Before it all. Her legs began vibrating as the dildo penetrated her. "Oh!" she moaned.

It took nearly ten minutes before she finally reached a powerful climax and was able to catch her breath. She set the soaked toy on the nightstand while Stephon kept on chanting, "beat that pussy up!" Then came a moment of silence.

"When you comin' to visit, Lex? I need to see you bad," he asked of her. "I need to talk to you about something real serious."

"Let me catch my breath!" she cooed. But before she could mumble anything else, there was a loud crashing noise coming from the living room followed by the sounds of footsteps clamoring across the hardwood floors of her two-bedroom condo. Paralyzed with fear, her mouth dangled open at the sight of two men in black jumpsuits and wearing ski masks as they came barging into her bedroom.

When she saw the Desert Eagle aimed at her head, she dropped the phone and that's when two sharp blows to the head knocked her unconscious. The larger of the two men started securing her wrists and the sounds of the duct tape being ripped from the spool sent chills of fear down Stephon's back as he

3

listened in. His screams fell upon deaf ears. Just then three more armed men who were speaking Spanish and some broken English entered the bedroom and began ransacking it.

"Lex! Lex! Alexis!" Stephon shouted into the phone just before his 15-minute call expired.

Chapter 2

Six years earlier...

It was a hot and sticky summer evening in the slums of St. Louis, Missouri, the sun just now setting in the western skies. In the streets, the demand for illicit drugs was at an all-time high, kilos of coke going for about 18-grand, while the city's homicide rate was climbing by the hour.

In one of the few newer homes in this neighborhood on Broadway Street, Alexis was doing her hair in front of the bathroom mirror and chewing bubble gum at the same time. She was twerkin', wearing a pair of yellow boy shorts with a white stripe running down both sides and a matching white cut-off wife beater with "Tweety Bird" stenciled mid-center. Her rose-tinted gold bangle earrings complimented the cute dimples on her face. In the master bedroom across the hallway from the bathroom, a newly released Nelly single blasted from her stereo system.

Standing only 4' 11" tall and weighing in at 136 pounds, Alexis had huge aspirations of locking down the extremely lucrative drug trade here in St. Louis; big dreams for such a small girl. Having been born and molded while growing up in New York, she was fearless and took chances that most men wouldn't even think of taking. Compared to New York, St. Louis was sweet as apple pie.

Her waist was unusually thin and amazingly for a Puerto Rican chick, her butt jumped and jiggled around like two volleyballs. She began sweating. "It's gettin' hot in here!" she sang, her New York accent coming through. She was still going at it, putting on a coat of pink lipstick, when she was startled by her young handsome boyfriend Danny who silently crept into view with a smirk on his face. He stood there watching her dancing around, her perky breasts shaking from side to side, the nipples hard and poking out. It appeared to him that she, too, was becoming aroused from looking at herself in the mirror.

"Damn, Lex, you got a whole lot of energy left, don't you, girl?" he asked, as he stood in the doorway with his arms crossed. He was holding a brown leather leash in one hand, at the end of which was a yellowish-red-colored pit bull puppy with big white paws. It was wagging its tail, looking up at her, and then it barked.

"Get that damn dog out my house!" she said, pointing down the carpeted hallway.

Danny frowned when he heard that order. "He too young to be outside. Somebody'll steal 'em!"

Alexis stormed out of the bathroom and rushed to the front door, unbolted the steel security door and pushed it open. Then she stood there with her hands on her hips, stone-faced as she looked into the eyes of an innocent kid. Danny had just turned nineteen a week earlier. He was a lanky kid of mixed heritage, his father Mexican and his mother black. He barely had a mustache, but the length and width of his penis was what mattered most to

Alexis. Plus, she believed she was training him to be loyal to her; her courageous soldier and a pawn. She'd recently taken his virginity from him, like snatching candy from a baby.

Danny eventually followed the puppy outdoors as it pulled him along. Alexis'eyes trailed after him, his pants sagging enough to expose the crack of his ass and the black Polo boxer shorts she'd recently bought him. She also noticed the black rubber grip from the .357 Magnum protruding from his rear pocket. Being nearly nine years older than him, she sometimes felt more like his mother than his lover.

He was pouting as he made his way around to the side of the house where the dog took a quick whiz. Then he heard a familiar growling noise that seemed to be getting louder, and when he glanced up Danny saw a Latino dude zooming down the street on a chrome and strawberry-red-colored Yamaha motorcycle. The guy pulled up and parked in front of an older house, then climbed off the custom-made bike. He appeared to be in fairly decent shape, a yellow-skinned pretty-boy type with braids hanging down to his shoulders and carrying a backpack. He was smiling when a short, thick and cute white girl came walking out of the house followed by two young black thugs, both wearing white T-shirts and long baggy shorts that hung to their ankles. One of them was wearing a blue bandanna over his dreadlocks and there were several other dudes on the front porch shooting dice and drinking beer. Alexis followed this dude's every move.

Now she pranced over to her white Mercedes that was parked in the shallow driveway and bent over as she reached in through the open passenger-side window. This created the sensation that her butt swallowed up the too-tight shorts she was wearing. Danny, meanwhile, was far too blind and immature to discern her ulterior motives. He was simply a boy in a young man's body. But his dick began to swell at the sight of her voluptuous ass, and a moment later the dude on the Yamaha shot by again going in the opposite direction, this time popping a wheelie damn near the entire length of the street. As he passed by her house, tooting his horn at Alexis, signaling to her that he'd noticed her. A cloud of fumes from the bike's exhaust clung in the air like fog, and the screaming sounds coming from the powerful motor could be heard blocks away. It was at that very moment that Alexis knew she had to have that dude.

Danny walked towards her. "Who the fuck's that, Lex? Huh?" he yelled over the sounds of the dog yapping who'd been chained to a six-foot privacy fence in the back.

"I don't know," she replied. "He's been back and forth for a few days. Either he's buying dope from them niggas or they buyin' from him."

Actually, Danny wasn't paying much attention to what she was saying. "Don't be out here bending over like that," he rambled on. "Let me pound that pussy out again befo' them junkies start comin' through," he told her while holding onto her arm.

She pulled her arm free. "Boy, you got my kitty cat sore. I'ma teach you how to eat my pussy tonight."

Twisting up his face at the nauseating thought, he said, "That'll never ever happen...hell nawww!"

Just then their heads turned when a silver Cadillac Escalade eased up to the curb, blocking in the Mercedes. It had tinted windows, so you couldn't see the driver. The 24-inch floaters were still spinning slow even though the SUV was parked. They were both staring at the truck, then smiled in unison when Danny's aunt Olivia climbed down from the driver's side. Alexis sashayed over to her and embrace the tall woman, each of them appearing excited to see the other. Olivia was a natural born hustler with long hair, brown skin and uniquely-shaped with long sculpted legs. She was covered in jewelry and wearing the hell out of a colorful Chanel skirt with matching peep-toe heels. And what was strange about her was the fact that she didn't even need to hustle. Drug dealers by the dozen tried to turn her into a housewife and take care of her, but she refused. When they'd get themselves arrested and eventually shipped off to prison, she would always maintain their connects and clientele. And make moves on their behalf, too. Word on the street was she had the best pussy in the entire Midwest. You couldn't tell if she was black or Latina.

"What up, auntie?" yelled Danny. "When you gone let me push your new truck?" he added with a smile but having no effect. Her wave to him in response was like always, without emotion. Olivia and Alexis were whispering amongst themselves, so Danny finally said, "Fuck it!" and went to untangle a nearby water hose, then filled his puppy's bowl with water.

When their conversation ended, Alexis dashed into the house and returned minutes later with her white Jimmy Choo purse slung over her shoulder. She saw Danny leaning on the door of the Caddy trying in vain to persuade his aunt to front him some dope. She wasn't hearing a word of it.

"Danny, I'ma be back. I left some weed in my dresser drawer, you know where," Alexis explained to him before climbing up into the passenger side of the Escalade, while Olivia first fumbled with her seatbelt, then the stereo.

As the truck coasted on up the street, Danny began pulling at his shorts, actually pulling them up. Just then he noticed a well-known neighborhood clucker headed his way, so he reached into his pocket and pulled out a plastic baggie full of yellow rocks. He quickly untied the knot, but to his surprise the dope fiend walked right on by him and went to the house up the street, the same place where the dude on the motorcycle had gone to earlier. And the same dudes and the white girl were sitting on the porch in the midst of a growing crowd. It looked to Danny as though the junky scored some dope, then headed in between two houses toward an alley and never resurfaced.

It was well over an hour before Alexis returned home, and clearly she was high. Danny was twisting and rolling his shoulders while thumbing a Playstation controller, playing NBA Live and smoking a blunt. His nickel-plated problem-solver rested beside him along with his pup.

"Where the hell you and auntie been?" he asked as he tossed the controller onto the leather sofa and stood up. The dog then moseyed over and sat down next to the front door and whined.

The first words out of Alexis's mouth were, "Get that goddamn dog out my house! You're going to make me give him some rat poison...keep on tryin' me!" She was carrying a plastic Walmart bag which she took into the kitchen and dumped out 9 ounces of crack - a quarter kilo, each ounce separately wrapped in clear sandwich bags. By the time Danny came back into the house, she'd hidden all but two ounces of the crack in a kitchen cabinet behind some 5-pound bags of flour and sugar. He never knew how much dope she was moving or buying, a rule that her brother had taught her at an early age back in the Bronx.

Danny stood in front of Alexis, looking down, waiting for an answer to the question he'd asked her before he took the dog outside. He noticed that her eyes were glassy looking. She turned to him and asked, "You see anybody out there? I need somebody to test this new shit out. Me and Olivia went in on it together."

"I'll see, but e'erybody been spendin' up the way. I ain't sold but a twenty bag."

"A twenty. That's it?"

"Yeah, that's all," he replied, lost now in her mysterious eyes. He began to feel like he'd failed in some way. His eyes were bloodshot from all the weed he'd been smoking, and when his puppy began barking he bolted out the front door.

And right behind him was Alexis. She watched Danny interact with some man she'd seen before. Her thoughts were impaired from the Vicodin pills she had popped with Olivia. She wanted to sit down, but she couldn't make herself pull her eyes away from Danny's youthfulness. Her desire boiled, her craving intensified, and her yearning for Danny's pelvic thrusts had her pussy twitching with anticipation.

Just then he came back into the house, bringing with him a tall, dark nappy-headed black guy. In addition to having what appeared to be only three teeth in his mouth, his lips were chapped and cracked, his skin looked ashen white, and he reeked of a putrid odor that nearly caused Alexis to vomit. She covered her mouth while the fiend stood there in the living room, scratching himself and admiring her immaculate furnishings.

"Y'all go out in the backyard," she ordered them. "Here, baby," she added, dropping a moist pebble of crack into Danny's hand. The crackhead and Danny then faded into the darkness behind the house.

The fiend was eager as he held his crack pipe in his hand, paranoia causing him to glance around the back yard. He was scaring the shit out of the young kid from the way his eyeballs were bulging from their deep-set eye sockets. He thought he looked like a monster, a crack monster at that. After he'd dropped a decent size rock in the clucker's hand, Danny started patting his pants pocket looking for his pistol. It wasn't there. It was still on the sofa. He swallowed hard. The experienced drug addict first struggled to strike his lighter, then finally the green lighter stayed lit long enough for him to hold it to the tip of the pipe where the Brillo was. He then placed the crack on the heated Brillo. It fizzled, melting instantly. Danny then thought about how the man's hands looked like those of some inhuman creature. All of his fingernails were either blackened or missing altogether.

The guy inhaled the fumes, holding the pipe to his lips as Danny looked on. White plumes of smoke were flowing through the milky-colored glass stem into his lungs. Then the hype just stood there smacking his teeth, eyes still roaming slowly, his nostrils flaring while smoke escaped through his mouth, then through his nose in slow motion. Danny began to sweat as the junky appeared angry.

12

"Sin...sin...sin," he mumbled. "Yep," he added, stepping closer to the boy. He frowned.

"Dis here's dat synthetic bullshit, boy. You sell dis to da wrong muddafucka, he will kill you! Take dis hera shit and trash it...ya hear me? Buy yaself some of dat good glass dem Crip niggas servin' up da screet, boy. Don't go flirt wit' death," he spat, before walking off. As he did, he disgruntledly removed the tainted Brillo from his crack pipe and threw it into a cluster of bushes nearby.

Chapter 3

Midnight had just rolled around and Olivia was coasting through the inner-city enroute to Alexis's house after discovering that the work she and Alexis had purchased together was garbage. Maybe during a drought, it might sell, but every hood in St. Louis was currently flooded with top-grade crack cocaine.

She'd been trying to call the dude who had sold it to them; some grimy cat she once fucked around with for the last hour, but to no avail. At a red light she snatched her cell phone from the console and tried again to reach him, but still no answer. She was now approaching Alexis' neighborhood.

In the meantime, in her darkened bedroom with a porno flick playing, Alexis' was teaching Danny all about the power of his tongue. She was certain that multiple orgasms would help to ease her frustration of suffering such a loss — five thousand dollars!

"Circle your tongue...yeah, right there...right there...harder...that's it! Mmmmnnn," she hissed, gripping his ears while gyrating her pelvis against his face...releasing again.

Danny finally came up for a breath of air, his face covered with white excretion from her pussy and cum from both of them.

He wiped his forearm across his chin, then his nose and lips, his throbbing dick brick hard and ready to fuck some more.

"What it taste like Danny?" she asked in a whisper as she gazed at his strong thick shaft. "Hmmm, vanilla?" Then she grabbed hold of it and began gently stroking it.

Gritting his teeth, he managed to groan, "Nothing like that. It taste like...uh, like...like shrimp or clams."

She choked back a laugh, while he took in her sexy naked body lying there. He began studying a rose tattoo on her hip as he ran his hand across her flat tummy, gently caressing her as he did. Her well-toned legs were spread wide open and trembling, as were the tender pink folds of her hairless pussy. Cum was still oozing from her, dripping down between her ass cheeks onto the black sheets.

Once their eyes made contact, he asked, "Why does it swell up like that? Is that your clit?" He was pointing at it, so she sat up a bit and glanced down at her fully erect clit, then laughed. But before she could respond, her cell phone began ringing. Danny reached over and grabbed her phone, then handed it to her. She answered the call while he tried to cuddle up next to her, but she gave him an elbow before jumping up and tossing the phone back onto the bed.

"Get dressed...hurry up!" she ordered him, snatching a rag from the foot of her bed and wiping herself between her legs and her crotch. "Olivia'll be here in a few minutes!"

They no sooner had gotten dressed than they heard a horn beep. Olivia had set the alarm on her truck. Alexis quickly peeked through her cherrywood blinds and saw Olivia in full stride headed

16

for the front door, the puppy barking at her like crazy from just outside her bedroom window.

"Go answer the door, Danny," she told him. "Wait!" she added, wiping his face. "She'd kill me knowing I'm fuckin' your young ass."

They both giggled and he tried to kiss her, but she shoved him up against a bedroom wall. Alexis simply wasn't into much affection. They'd never kissed or held hands, never nothing like that.

Now Olivia and Alexis were sitting at a marble dining room table discussing just how they were going to handle the situation. It was all too obvious that they'd been burned. Alexis tossed around the idea of burning someone else with the same dope, but Olivia didn't seem too interested in doing that.

Meanwhile, Danny was listening to the conversation and becoming obsessed with the thought of fixing the problem himself. He knew about the dude called Sugar Man who they were talking about and knew that he hung out over in East St. Louis, Illinois. In fact, he recalled seeing the dude at his fine-ass baby momma's crib in the Gompers housing projects on 6th and Martin Luther King Drive. Danny's older cousin CC on his mother's side lived just a few apartments down from her. It's like when you're getting real money in the streets everybody knows you, wants to know you, or pretends to know you.

Danny finally stood up, his chest puffed out, and walked into the dining room. "I know where that pussy nigga be at," he told them in a tough-guy sort of way."Yeah, I'll handle his ass for you, auntie, you need me to."

Olivia looked over at him while pulling hard on her cigarette, then smashed the cherry in an octagon-shaped glass ashtray. There were three candles burning atop the center of the table creating shadows that danced across the white walls. Thick cigarette smoke still lingered in the air as a brief moment of solitude fell upon them. Everyone was quiet, which is when Danny inched up beside Alexis. "I know where his baby momma stay at. Yep! Down from CC's apartment."

"Where?" asked Alexis. "Who's CC, your people?"

Then Olivia chimed in, anger written all over her face. "Danny, don't you see grown bitches talkin'? So shut the fuck up!"

"Wait, Olivia, let 'em speak," replied Alexis. "We need all the leads we can get. I ain't got no money to donate to no sorry black motherfucka! And what made you wanna go shop with him anyway? We been getting straight with J-Rock."

"W-what're you tryin' to say, Lex? You think I got something to do wit' it, don't you? I lost five grand, too honey, just like you!"

"No, I didn't insinuate nothing like that. You just did, Olivia."

Danny sat down at the head of the exquisitely-made table. Before speaking his mind, however, he stared over at a large wood-framed picture of Jesus and his twelve disciples that was mounted on the dining room wall. "Hold on, y'all, don't argue. I can take y'all right to his baby momma's crib. Sugar Man's got three kids over there," he explained, frowning.

Alexis glanced over at her young man and reasoned, "I think we do need to take a quick ride over to Gompers, girl, see if we can find this bitch nigga."

Olivia didn't reply to the suggestion, instead fired up another cigarette. She appeared to be somewhat nervous as she tapped her French-tipped nails on the marble tabletop while glaring scornfully at Danny. Finally, she decided to break the silence and exhaled a large grey plume of smoke.

"Look, Danny," she said, then began coughing before she continued. "I don't want you involved in this shit. Yo' mama, my big sister, would roll over in her grave if I get you jammed up out her in these streets. I love you, boy!"

"Auntie, I ain't no li'l boy no more. Don't you see, I'ma man?"

When Olivia refused to acknowledge his manhood, Alexis roared, "Danny, let's go! Show me where this fag's people live. Bet ya I'm not scaaared...I'm 'bout this shit!"

He stood up, followed by Olivia, while Alexis stormed off into her bedroom. She returned quickly with her purse, clutching the key to her Benz and her cell phone. Then she leaned over and blew out the candles on the dining room table before heading towards the front door.

"I'll follow behind y'all," quipped Olivia.

"Don't even worry 'bout it, girl. He might see your truck and go further underground," Alexis told her, then gently grabbed hold of her arm. "I'll call you in the morning if we see him. 'Livia, go home, get yourself some sleep. You look tired."

"Okay...I am tired, Lex. I'm sorry this happened."

Meanwhile, it was Danny's knowledge of Sugar Man's baby momma's apartment that earned him the right to keep his precious puppy in the bathroom until they returned home.

And while Alexis sat in the driveway behind the woodgrain steering wheel of her car waiting for Danny, she looked up and noticed the influx of traffic just down the block from where she was sitting. There seemed to be a steady flow of customers, a crowd really, mostly younger college-looking kids pulling up to get curbside service, driving new vehicles. She pondered this as she watched the same jazzy-looking white girl walk out to the cars at the curb, serve them and walk back onto the porch, then hand the money she'd collected to some guy who dashed into the house.

Alexis didn't even bother waving goodbye to Olivia as the dark-tinted window slid back up and the truck pulled off. Danny crawled into the passenger side of the Benz with a lit blunt in his hand and they rolled off, too. Olivia and Alexis eventually going separate ways at a stop light not far from her house.

During the 15-minute ride across the bridge on the way to the projects, Danny was quiet, keeping his thoughts to himself. As did Alexis. They passed the strong blunt back and forth; total silence in the car with no music playing. Danny's thoughts took him back to the time when he and Alexis traveled to New York for a 3-day trip. He recalled now the area where they partied being called Soundview. Suddenly, that unforgettable image of him fucking Alexis in an expensive penthouse suite overlooking downtown Manhattan came to mind. Those lullaby thoughts aroused his senses as he glanced over at her thin but strong thighs, then her crotch. He could still smell the sweet scent from her vagina on his fingers.

But then his mind's moment of delight came to an abrupt end when he looked up and saw Sugar Man standing in front of a candy-painted '72 Cutlass convertible with two other guys turning up 40s. He squinted, confirming his observations, seeing that Sugar Man was wearing a black Dickie outfit and holding onto his small son's hand who was standing next to him. Nothing unusual at this time of night in the hood. The boy looked to be no more than three or four years old and people were hanging out everywhere.

"Wait, Lex, let me out...stop!" yelled Danny.

Alexis carefully eased the wide-bodied Mercedes over the yellow curb trying not to scrape the chrome rims against the curb in Gompers housing projects. But before she could even come to a stop, he leaped from the car leaving the door ajar, then quickly slithered in behind a large U-Haul truck sitting in the parking lot.

"Danny!" she hollered. "Where?"

But he wasn't waiting. Danny had a dark destiny of his own. Subconsciously, he'd been waiting for this very moment his entire young life. He had something to prove, to himself, to Lex, to the guys he grew up with. It was about earning his keep in Alexis's heart. A reputation on the streets...and just maybe a portion of that 10 grand! The thought of all this is what drove him, it was his motivation. In fact, he was inspired like never before in his entire life as he tightly clutched the grip of his pistol in the darkness while in full stride.

Meanwhile, Alexis killed the engine, then the headlights. A moment later she jumped in fear when she heard the six consecutive explosions pierce the heavy night air. She heard muffled screams nearby and saw a prostitute scurry across a gangway. Then Danny came sprinting from around an adjacent

21

two-story building carrying a black tote bag, his pistol, and a diamond and platinum chain that sparkled like glitter under the dim glow coming from a street light. He could barely speak straight and Alexis's hands were shaking, then he pulled the door shut and pounded on the dashboard—BOOM!

"Bitch, take off!" he screamed, then he looked back through the rear window. A man dressed in all black was in hot pursuit on foot and closing the distance fast. Just then one of the four shots he fired shattered a rear window panel on her Mercedes as she floored it!

Navigating as cautiously as she could through the cold-hearted streets of East St. Louis, searching for a way out...a way home. She turned left on 6th Street...

Chapter 4

In the hood, murder has a wicked and mystserious way of spreading faster than a contagious disease, a fact that Danny had obviously neglected to take into account on this night. He exhaled, emitting a deep sigh of relief, hoping to calm his nerves as he stared at the house. Then he wiped some of the speckles of dried blood from his face. He and Alexis were still sitting in the Mercedes parked in the darkened driveway in front of her house. She glanced over her shoulder at the back seat and the shards of glass scattered all over the leather seats and carpet.

Danny was still coming out of his trance-like state as he began to slowly rifle his hand through the bag resting on his lap, at the same time mounting the spoils of revenge around his neck. The flashy chain with the cross medallion dangled down to his stomach.

Alexis just stared at him with a sort of fury infused with curiosity. Suddenly, Danny pulled out two tight-fisted bundles of cash. He kissed the blood money and dropped it back into the bag, then removed a larger than usual Ziploc bag containing what appeared to be a dozen ounces of purple-colored weed, coke and crack. But he kept digging further, to the bottom, until he felt a solid object, which just happened to be a sub-compact Springfield Armory .40 Caliber. He pulled that out and kissed it too, wearing a heroic-looking smirk on his face before sliding the gun into his front pocket.

Alexis continued staring at him.

"Tol' y'all I'd get y'all's loot back, didn't I?" he boasted while rocking back and forth. He pulled up some more cash out from the bag, biting his bottom lip.

Without warning, she slapped his face and screamed, "Your stupid ass could've gotten me killed! Are you fucking crazy?"

Holding a hand to his face, he sputtered, "You the one kept on cryin' 'bout g-g-gettin' burnt an' all. I-I mean, a nigga beatin' y'all out–"

"Tell me what the fuck just happened back there!" she demanded; her arms folded across her chest. She was spooked half to death as she glanced around the dark neighborhood. Then an older-model car crept by and parked two houses down the block, its brakes screeching before it came to a complete stop. They feared it was the cops.

But it wasn't.

Danny didn't respond, rubbing his cheek as he sat there dazed in murderous reflection. Then Alexis punched him on the arm and yelled, "Are you bleeding?"

Rubbing his chest now, he told her, "I'm good," then closed his eyes. "I swear I told the stupid motherfuckers not to move! But he picks up the li'l boy...his son, holdin' 'im up like a bulletproof shield...piece of hot shit! Then one of his guys lowered his arms, reaching around behind his back, so...so I popped his head open.

24

And I-I-I kept on squeezin'...fuck nigga, Sugar Man tried to run to his droptop...I let 'im have it! Stretched his black ass out...it all happened so fast."

"You said li'l boy. What happened to a li'l boy?" she asked, her eyes tearing up at the thought.

"I shot 'im in the head first, I told you."

Alexis covered her mouth with her hand. "Why...why'd you kill a child, Danny...why?"

"Fuck you mean? Ain't no rules to dis here shit, Lex. Nigga loved 'is family so much, he was 'posed to been moved 'em to the 'burbs. The third nigga dives underneath a car, right? He let off a round, it ricocheted off the ground near my feet. So I jumped up in Sugar's whip, grabbed this bag sitting on the back seat and jetted! But before I did, I squeezed two mo' slugs in Sugar's hardheaded ass and I snatched this." He held up the chain that glittered, then let it fall against his chest. "The stupid motherfucka under the car began chasing me. I didn't realize I ran out of bullets..."

Alexis was listening, and crying. She even rested her head on his shoulder while he ran his fingers through her soft lustrous hair. Suddenly, she pushed his hand away and sat up. She was thinking about her daughter up in New York who was relying on her to pay for her private schooling. Alexis was thankful that her daughter was safe and well-protected from the type of lifestyle she'd chosen for herself. For just a moment she considered the implications of being an accomplice to the murders, then her thoughts were interrupted when her cell phone rang.

She glanced at the screen. "It's Olivia," she sniffled. "I don't know if I should even answer it." So she didn't. She simply pressed a red button on the keypad, sending Olivia to voicemail. It immediately rang again, so she turned it off.

Danny wrapped his arm around Alexis, holding her next to him as he walked her to the front door. She keyed the security door and was just turning the doorknob to the second door when Danny suddenly dropped the tote bag and nearly shoved her to the ground. He reached into his pocket and brought up his pistol, aiming it at the naked white girl who'd come running up the street into their yard! She was frantic, crying and holding her hands up, gasping for air! Then slowly she dropped her hands to cover her full breasts.

"Somebody's robbing my friend's house! Please, help me...p-please... Help m-me!" she cried out very convincingly.

But before Alexis or Danny could react or even say anything, they heard a series of automatic gunfire, machine gun-like blasts, coming from up the block, followed by a few more reports echoing in the night. Alexis was squatting down as she pushed the door open and motioned for the young blond-haired girl to follow her inside. Once they were safely inside, Alexis slammed the door shut, leaving Danny outside scurrying for cover.

He was standing around the corner of the house under a blanket of darkness as he observed two light-skinned goons peeling off ski masks as they ran towards a late-model green Monte Carlo. One dude was carrying an AK-47 while the other one struggled with what appeared to be a heavy trash bag. They leaped inside the car and burned rubber as they pulled away until

26

they reached a side street, turned left, sideswiped a parked car and disappeared into the night with their headlights off.

Danny stood there thinking that he'd seen the driver somewhere before, but after the bloody night's work he'd just put in, his state of mind was too scrambled to place where. And it didn't really matter to him anyway. He was just praying that he wouldn't be identified as the killer of those two men and a guiltless child. As he picked up the bag containing the cash and narcotics, he tried to rid himself of those seemingly feminine-like emotions.

As soon as he got inside the house, Alexis started yelling at him to get his puppy out of the bathroom. It was tied to the faucet in the bathtub, its leash in knots now, and there was dog shit everywhere — inside the tub and even on the toilet. The naked white girl, who told Alexis her name was Becky, had to pee, bad, and was doing her best to hold it in, while Danny used his T-shirt to wipe dog shit off the floor.

When Alexis returned from her bedroom with a towel and a long white shirt for Becky, the girl was squatting down in the hallway, her thighs spread wide open. She slowly, and methodically removed a large baggie containing several hundred multi-colored tablets that had been rolled up and inserted in her pussy. She carefully wiped the bag with her hand, and sniffed it once, then unrolled it.

As they stood and watched, both Danny and Alexis asked, "What's that?" in the same breath.

Becky grinned and stood up, then tiptoed barefoot into the bathroom. She sat down on the toilet to pee while the excited pup wagged its tail and licked at her feet and toes. She didn't seem to mind it at all, not even the horrible stench permeating the air in the small bathroom. There were beads of sweat on her pale ivory-colored face. She was maybe 22-years old at most, Alexis thought, and as pretty as a morning sunrise.

"This is ecstasy, girl," she finally answered. "Nothing in the world sells like this stuff girl," she added, looking at both of them. It didn't seem as though Becky realized or even cared that she was naked and pissing in front of total strangers. Then she asked, "Can I use your phone to call my man to come pick me up?"

Alexis tossed her the shirt and towel while Danny stood there in the doorway with his mouth open, drooling over Becky's uninhibited nature. He watched while she wiped her vagina with a wad of toilet paper and felt his manhood swelling fast. At the same time he began to wonder about the effects of the colorful tablets she was holding. To him they looked like candy... Skittles.

Not surprisingly, no one even thought of, or seemed to care at all about the status of Becky's friends, their safety or their fate. And the idea of calling the cops never occurred to anyone because in the ghetto, police, lawyers and judges are deemed to be colder, if not feared more than the so-called criminal element itself.

Several hours later, after having thoroughly cleaned the bathroom, Danny now rung out the mop and jumped in the shower. He was so proud of himself that he didn't even bother removing the very expensive platinum and diamond chain from around his neck as the hot water pelted his body. He cringed, however, as splotches of dried blood that had hardened and caked onto the back of the cross medallion dissolved and flowed down his stomach into the drain. And he'd been aware enough of his situation and had the good street-sense to take the murder weapon— the .357 Mag — out to the alley and toss it up on the roof of an abandoned house.

Birds were just now starting to chirp, the beautiful day beginning to feel much like a prosperous one indeed...to Danny. Alexis and Becky seemed to be enjoying each other's company. Which was unusual because Alexis didn't like meeting new people, and on principle alone, kept a small tight cadre of associates in St. Louis. She served a handful of dudes who peddled drugs hand-to-hand on street corners and kept the company of a few heavyweights from up top who trafficked in guns and bricks, all the way from New York to St. Louis.

After stashing his dope and money in a closet, Danny crept into the living room shirtless and caught Becky's lustful eye, just like he'd hoped to. She was sipping a glass of water as she began punching numbers in Alexis's phone while Alexis was flicking a remote control at the TV mounted on a wall. Music flowed from the CD in Danny's Playstation 2, the volume lowered as Becky stood up and peeked out through the blinds on the living room window. The phone was to her ear as she spoke.

"Chino, what's taking you so long?" she asked, pausing for a reply.

With bloodshot eyes and lids drooping, Alexis looked like she was about to fall asleep, as she curled up into a fetal position on the sofa. Danny was eager for her to doze off as he eyeballed Becky's juicy wide round ass, knowing full well that she wasn't wearing any panties under the white shirt she had on. Her calves were shaved and shapely. He began breaking up some of Sugar Man's purple in a Backwoods cigar.

"There isn't any po-leese out here, honey. I hate to feel like I'm intruding on this nice couple. They been welcoming to me. Chino, are you close?" she asked. Hanging her head, Becky tried to extend the phone to Alexis whose eyes were shut now, mouth open and softly snoring.

"She fell asleep...don't wake 'er!" whispered Danny. He quickly grabbed the phone and set it on the end table, then nodded towards the hallway. Softly he whispered, "Let's go talk in the bathroom." She reached down and grabbed her glass of water, then followed him to the bathroom.

When he'd locked the bathroom door behind them, Becky jumped and sat on the vanity countertop. Danny passed her the blunt, she hit it once, coughed, and began masterbating with two fingers right before his very eyes! Her pussy was hairy and wet, and hot pink. It was like a fantasy, but unfortunately one that was easily dispelled by the familiar scream of an approaching motorcycle.

Becky leaped down off the countertop. "My man's here!" she said excitedly before giving Danny a quick kiss on his forehead, then running back into the living room. "Alexis...my boyfriend's here...wake up!"

Alexis awoke and her eyes snapped open, bringing her back to reality when she heard the puppy barking followed by the sound of the bike's motor revving up a few times before it died.

Next Becky poured out about a hundred or more ecstasy tablets onto an end table in the living room, then grabbed Alexis's hand. "Come meet him...c'mon, girl," she pleaded. "Bye Danny. Those are for y'all. It's the very least I can do to show my appreciation. I'll be in touch, Alexis, I promise."

Danny trailed after the ladies until they got outside, all the while still puffing away on the powerful blunt. He stood there staring at the dude as he dismounted the chromed-out bike that gleamed from the reflection of the early morning sun rising in the east. He decided that he really wasn't interested in the guy, so he left to tend to the needs of his pup.

Alexis, however, was utterly speechless. To her this dude was a god! Her heart raced as she gazed into his penetrating brown eyes.

He seemed a little nervous, though, like he was trying to look in all directions at the same time. Suddenly, it came to Danny: this was the same dude who'd been carrying the AK-47 just hours earlier. The same Jordans, same braid design in his hair, the one who had made off in the Monte Carlo. He watched the guy dig in his pocket to retrieve his cell phone and enter Alexis's phone number as she gave it to him. Then he wrestled out a hefty bankroll and placed a pile of bills in her hand.

She was in love.

"Give ya man half of that, ma," he told her, "and thanks for keepin' my chick out of harm's way."

"Uh...okay, no problem. But you need to take better care of your girl," she suggested in a condescending tone of voice.

"Damn, ma, you don't even know me. But they call me Chino. Listen, we gots to go. Get with me ifyou need work. I got whatever. Ain't no order too big."

Becky was smiling and waving her goodbyes to Alexis and Danny as she mounted the bike, straddling the seat behind Chino and grabbing hold of his lean midsection. Her entire ass was exposed as the bike accelerated and growled on down the street.

Danny and Alexis just stood there watching until the bike was out of sight while dope fiends aimlessly roamed the street. Some were carrying stereos, CD players, one struggled carrying an air-conditioner, another had a television, each of them coming from the house up the block. The stench of death was hanging in the air.

Before either of them could go back inside, Olivia's Cadillac came screeching around the corner and skidded to an abrupt halt in front of the house, dust flying everywhere. Olivia's brother Harold, Danny's uncle, scurried out of the SUV and ran straight up to Danny. He grabbed him by the front of his shirt, punched his skinny ass to the ground, then kicked him in the ribs, twice! Next, he turned to the barking dog and kicked it, sending it on a voyage head first into the fence. He leaned over and snatched Danny by the hair. "Go get your shit, boy," he ordered him. "You goin' with me...tell your pretty girlfriend goodbye!" Uncle Harold was built like a tree stump and bald headed with muscles on top of muscles. It looked as if all he ever did was pump iron, in and out of the state joint.

Danny stumbled into the house, his nose dripping blood and Alexis following behind, crying.

Harold jumped back into the truck to make a call on his cell phone. The man was all black, with zero tolerace, and no interracial cut. A menacing looking dude, he stood nearly six-three and was dark as tar. He only knew how to deal with situations using swift violence.

Meanwhile, trying desperately not to cry himself, in front of Alexis, Danny was busy packing his clothes. In a generous gesture, he handed her a few bundles of his cash, then stashed his pistol in the bag. She turned and ran to the kitchen, then returned with the quarter key of bullshit Sugar Man had sold her. "You want this?" she asked him.

"Yeah." He tossed it in the bag just before he looked up and saw Harold's shadow on the wall, then his bloodshot eyes as he rounded the corner. "Come on, little motherfucka!" When Harold turned to Alexis, Danny swiftly swiped a fistful of the ecstasy pills that had been lying on the end table and covertly pocketed them.

Now Harold was looking down at Alexis's sexy little frame as he tried to explain. "We hidin' him out. I apologize. We do not wanna see him spendin' the rest of his life in the penitentiary...like me. I spent my whole life on the chain gang."

"Where's Olivia at?" asked Alexis.

"She at the hospital with CC. Somebody shot her in the head last night. We tryin' to get to the bottom of this. CC probably won't make it. It seems to be retaliation for what Danny did last night."

Chapter 5

With Uncle Harold navigating the Escalade and Danny riding shotgun, they were coasting smoothly along Highway 61, South, bound for Southern Illinois. They'd been driving for more than half-an-hour while Harold barked out orders on his cell phone to several different people, speaking a slang that Danny had never heard before, that is, except for dollar amounts.

Meanwhile, he was busy tenderly nursing a swollen lip as he peered into the sunvisor mirror on the passenger side. As he was doing this, it became apparent that Harold was just informed over his phone that CC had died from her injuries at St. Mary's Hospital.

Uncle Harold ended his call with Olivia. For the next ten minutes he was as quiet as a dark country night. Suddenly, he reached over and turned off the stereo. "Nephew, CC ain't pull through. She gone. I really feel like beatin' the fuck out of yo' trigger-happy, half-breed punk ass. But I know how it is in these streets. I'm a street nigga. Always have been, except for when I was doin' time in Menard. Fuck! Sometimes you got to react wit'out thinkin' 'bout the consequences of yo' actions...how they affect other people's lives. I killed my first nigga 'bout yo' age, too, 'cept I got caught. Red-handed. You killed three folks. Good thing ain't nobody caught you...yet."

Danny was barely paying attention, his mind drifting off to Alexis, to poor CC, then his dog. From the corner of his eye he watched his uncle while his big pink lips kept flapping up and down. He was musty, too. A white wife-beater covered his barrel-shaped chest and his arms looked more like thighs, rippled with veins and covered with prison tattoos that were hard to see because of his shiny skin and dark complexion. Danny was recalling his visits with Harold, ten maybe twelve years ago while he was in prison, but damn, his uncle had grown so much since then. And while he had great respect for Harold, at the moment his lip and his nose hurt like a motherfucker. And looked deformed! he thought.

"You listenin' to me, punk?" roared Harold as he slammed the sunvisor shut.

"Yeah, Uncle Harold. Man..." he replied, startled from his reverie. "Why'd you have to kick my puppy?"

Harold froze with a puzzled look on his face. Danny's question struck him as odd, especially since Danny could be facing decades in prison, possibly even life. Questioningly, he glanced over at the kid, the blue-tinted diamonds on the chain hanging from his neck sparkling and dancing in sync with the sun's rays as they shone through the windshield. The young man was awaiting his response while Harold was reminded of how they were alike in so many ways. After all, they were blood, he considered, then told him, "That dog was a mutt...just like you!"

The silence continued as they cruised through the small town of Chester. "I'm sorry, nephew. Listen, I got seventy-five or eighty game dogs if that's what you're so pissed off at me 'bout. I figured you'd be mad 'bout that fat lip of yours and that pretty bitch you left behind. Huh? You fuckin' her?"

That brought a grin to Danny's face and he tried to hide it. "Yeah, that's my bitch. She older than me," he explained, then added, "but I only like pit bulls. That was a red nose! I wish you would've let me bring 'im wit' us."

Harold studied him for a moment, then said, "Nephew, didn't I just tell you that was a fuckin' mutt, huh? Now, this is what it is. When we get to my farm, yo' job gone be to work wit' REAL pit bulls, nigga. You work fo' me! I'm yo' boss. Fuck if I let them white prison asshole guards work you to death. I'm yo' boss, ya hear me li'l young nigga?"

"Yeah."

"Maybe in time we'll set it up fo' you to get to see ya gal. Come visit you for a few days. That's if she the type who keeps her gotdamn mouth shut, and legs closed. Not many of them..."

For the next thirty-minutes Danny ignored Uncle Harold and silently enjoyed watching the countryside as they drove along. He could see miles and miles, row upon row of corn and wheat fields, cattle, barns and silos, all of which riddled the country road they were traveling on.

*****

He had decided to spend the night at one of his stash houses. As he stood at the stove in the kitchen, wearing only his boxer shorts,

Chino was vigorously stirring the tip from a broken fishing pole into a deep Pyrex glass pot until the fish-scaled cocaine boiled and liquefied into a golden-colored gel-like substance. If you didn't know exactly what he was doing, you'd think he was scrambling eggs. The soul-seducing fumes he inhaled from the "cook-up" always made him horny. His dick was hard as iron and in need of Becky's care, but she was still asleep.

After pulling the pot off the stove, Chino dropped a few dozen ice cubes into the lucrative poison. Then, as he was weighing the yellowish-colored cake-like bricks of crack and separating them into four piles of 252 grams each, he suddenly began having flashbacks, visions of blood gushing like a geyser from the bullet hole in the head of one of the guys he'd shot. Damn! he thought to himself. He loved committing murder with the AK-47, it always left a grotesque mess of blood and mangled flesh in the aftermath of a shooting. He was hoping to upgrade soon from the dual-flippable banana clips to a higher capacity drum.

And in the back of his mind, he was wrestling with one inescapable question: Why Becky failed to follow his instructions and ran to the house belonging to that smart-mouthed little Puerto Rican girl instead of going to the Monte Carlo. He was certain that the bodies would be discovered by now and would be at the local mortuary in a few days. All closed caskets, of course.

After drying, one of the quarter keys, which was 252 grams worth, came up short by a few grams; nothing unusual in this trade. So, with a razorblade Chino chopped the dope down on a black plate into a bunch of ten-dollar rocks the size of

Lemonheads. Those would be sold at his dime spot by his foot soldiers on the Westside of St. Louis.

It was no secret that Chino was a true street animal, young and ruthless and very dangerous. If he didn't like you, he'd sell you a few bricks, let you get them off, then come back the next day and rob you of your cash and all the dope still left and kill you. After that he'd call an army of his guys down from Chicago to take over your block. He wasn't real fond of St. Louis niggas anyway, labeling them as "cut throats" and "back stabbers" of the worst kind. So he used, misused and abused them accordingly to his benefit.

Just as he was about to cook up the third bird, in walked Becky to the cluttered kitchen, naked, gorgeous, and still sleepy-eyed. When he stood up she reached up to hug him, then as they embraced he grabbed hold of her warm ass cheeks, pulling them apart, and began kissing both of her perky, hard, pink little nipples.

Meanwhile, there was well over three-hundred thousand in cold cash piled up like three mountains on a cheap-looking brass and glass light oak dining room table...the night's take.

"Chino, I love you," mumbled Becky.

He knew full well that it was going to be a busy day and he wanted to bust off a good nut before it all began. In such a short-term profession, you just never knew what to expect because death was always out there lurking around the corner. Prison, too. Therefore, most street hustler's minds are conditioned to "get it while the gettin's good." And live without remorse or regrets.

As if she was reading his cunning mind, Becky dropped to her knees in between his pale-yellow hairy thighs and began sucking him off. Slowly at first, the head of his dick swelling up like a fat mushroom in her sensual mouth. Chino was staring up at the ceiling, his mouth wide open, and before long his eyes closed.

"Bitch, you'se a beast...shit!" he declared as he gazed down into her hypnotizing blue eyes, while she hummed. This didn't last but a few minutes because he heard the sound coming from someone's car stereo system as it began vibrating the glass table. Then he heard the car pull into the gravel driveway out front at about the same time his cell phone began to vibrate, sitting on the table.

"Mmm...shit! Girl, hold up," he cried out as he glanced at the phone's Caller ID.

From behind the closed front door, someone yelled, "It's me!" And just by the tone of voice, Chino knew it was his main man, Kilo. Before darting back to the bedroom, Becky grabbed a bottle of water from the refrigerator.

As was their custom when greeting each other, they both threw up pitchforks formed with their fingers and hands, then slapped palms before sitting down at the table. Kilo's kinky afro stood straight up in the air, defying the law of gravity, because he only had two braided corn rows on one side of his head.

They'd known each other ever since their early days in the juvenile center back in Chicago. "You take care of the car?" Chino asked Kilo, trying to situate his dick as it deflated.

"I dowsed it wit' gas and set it ablaze, my nigga. The choppers are safe and put up."

"Good. Good," Chino smiled, slowly sliding him a third of the piles of money. "This your share, Kilo, a hundred and two thou. Don't spen' it all in one spot," he laughed, alluding to Kilo's expensive gambling addiction.

"Yeah, yeah, yeah. My nigga, what about the cane?"

"Easy," he stated, rubbing a hand across his face. "You gone have to cook your own shit. I ain't have the time, bruh. I was gettin' brains when you pulled up."

"I guess you ain't been home, huh?"

Chino shook his head, then reached over and grabbed a hold of a bird that was sittin on a chair beside him, still wrapped in the original packaging. "Melissa's gone be actin' a goddamn fool. But all I got to do is send her shoppin' or bring her home somethin' sparklin'."

They both got a big laugh out of that, then Kilo asked, "You figure out why ol' girl wasn't in da car waiting? I thought she went bad on us." He was scratching at his head trying to untangle his hair.

"I did, too. But as she explained, there was a couple outside and she didn't wanna bring

no heat or eyeballs to the getaway car. Which was good thinkin'."

"You believe her, Chino? C—"

"Nigga, if I didn't, she would've been burnt to a crisp in the trunk of that Monte. This young bitch's special! I almost wanna send her back to law school, get 'er off the street scene...and especially off them X pills she loves so fuckin' much. She would make one hell of a lawyer. We might need one someday, you know?"

"Money ova bitches, Chino. Neva forget that," he told him, then stood up and started gathering up his portion of the money. "And I'm not feelin' that pussy ass comment about needin' no lawyers—fuck dat! I'm holdin' court in the streets! Neva see me in no courtroom beggin' no cracker for a lighter sentence. Or workin' in nobody's mess hall wipin' tables!"

Becky had been eavesdropping from the bedroom and quickly popped two more double-stacked pink superwoman tablets.

And Kilo was pissed off at Chino, shouting now, "MOB, nigga! Don't get soft on me and start talkin' 'bout no lawyers and court!"

Just then Chino's cell phone began vibrating once again. He clutched it and said, "Yo, who dis?" then paused for a moment."What's good, Alexis?" he snickered into the phone. "Yeah...ma, I remember you. I'm always straight." He paused again smiling. "A nine-piece fried chicken dinner's going for forty-five...for you, forty-two."

Kilo was methodically putting away all of his money into a nearby trash bag, counting bundle after bundle, then placing the brick on top of all that. And he was still cussing in a whisper as to how he felt about lawyers. Suddenly, he pulled out his 9-milly from his waist and jacked a live round into the chamber. "Fuck a muthafuckin' cop! Lawyer! Judge! And warden!" Chino was smiling after he ended the call. "Calm down, fool! I shouldn't have brought the shit up," he told him as he patted Kilo on the back.

Kilo was staring at all the boxes of baking soda that had been spilled all over the counter. Then a bottle of Grey Goose vodka caught his eye. They made a toast and began a game of chess. A cloud hovered in the air above them as Kilo sat there babysitting a thick blunt. He slid his black queen across the board with a smirk on his face.

In response, Chino moved a pawn and said, "Earlier, that was a little chick from last night. I think I'ma put this bad li'l broad on. I like her gangsta. That whole block's ours. You know that, right?"

"Checkmate, nigga!" growled Kilo. "Stay focused!"

With that said, Chino knocked over all the chess pieces and stood up. "Yeah, no doubt. But check this out. I'm goin' to the city t'night. I need to put the icin' on the cake...the big-ass ecstasy deal. You stay here and keep e'erybody supplied.

This shit plays out how I calculated it to, we'll see a couple mill in only a matter of a few months. Ya hear me? Them rich college kids crazy 'bout that X. So what you think the niggas in the hood gone do when they get hooked, hmmm? We gone be rolling in the dough, nigga—filthy rich!"

Kilo grabbed his trash bag, glanced at his watch, then downed the rest of his vodka and rattled the ice cubes in his glass a few times. "'Rolling huh, Chino?" He smiled. "I like the sound of dat."

Chino smiled back, suddenly realizing that the trail of tattooed teardrops underneath Kilo's right eye seemed to be getting longer. "I'll get at you when I get back in town tomorrow," he assured his main man as he walked him to the front door.

*****

43

In reality, Chino's better judgment had warned him against delivering Alexis's order, the quarter key of rock to her house and instead have her meet him someplace, like Union Station.

At Regal Package Liquor Store on 18th and State Street, he very smoothly handed two of his underlings half a brick each, then climbed back up into his triple-black Yukon XL which was perched on some 23-inch blinding chrome Lexani rims. Like a chainsaw, Chino cut through lunch-hour traffic while a Young Jeezy CD beat through his eight 15-inch subwoofers. Much like the Flowmaster exhaust on his truck, he too was screaming, "Let's get it!" when he turned off Broadway and parked directly in front of Alexis's house. Her snow-white Benz was there. For a few seconds he just sat there staring back up the block, lost in thought, or maybe guilt, after having a sudden flashback. Then he shut off the stereo and the engine.

There was a dark-green Crown Victoria parked down in front of the house. Yellow crime-scene tape was all around the crib. And a woman in a business suit taking pictures of the house. He glanced in his rearview mirror and immediately spotted a convoy of law enforcement vehicles with their headlights on heading in his direction. With the appearance of being very calm, he snatched the brown paper bag containing the dope and crammed it down the front of his underwear, securing it neatly beneath his balls. Then just before leaping down from his SUV, Chino quickly slid his Ruger under the passenger-side seat. Beads of sweat were forming across his forehead and his nose, his braids swinging back and forth as he made his way across the yard where the puppy was pitifully scratching at an empty bowl.

Knock-Knock-Knock!

Four, then five...no, six squad cars shot past followed by two white cargo-style coroner vans creeping along. Shit! Hurry the fuck up, he though while standing there. Then he heard what sounded like door locks coming unbolted. "Hurry up, ma!"

She pushed open the front door and peered out. "What's going on out there?"

"Po-pos must be doin' a raid. I don't know." He stepped inside.

When she shut and bolted the door, it sounded like prison locks, thought Chino. He moved over in front of the window blinds and peeked out. Alexis was clad in only a slinky pink silk gown with spaghetti straps across her shoulders. She gave off a scent that smelled like some kind of exotic tropical fruit.

"Ain't them yo' people they're raiding?"

No!"

"Yeah, right."

They were both standing there peeking through the miniblinds when he eased in behind her to get a better view from a right angle. His hand brushed softly against the silky garment she was wearing and the next thing she knew was when his hand slid around her firm waist, cuffing her rear end. She snapped back from her reverie and, although she was enjoying how he touched her, she told him, "Get your hands off my ass!" then slapped his hand away. "You got my stuff?" she asked.

"Yeah, I got you. Can I sit down?"

"Go 'head."

With goose bumps she shivered as she watched him stride toward her sofa. He sat down and began digging around in his well-fittin black Red Monkey jeans. Seconds later he pulled out the brown paper bag and slowly poured out the product onto a cocktail table, all neatly wrapped in clear sandwich bags. She sat down on the loveseat across from him and inspected each cookie very carefully, turning them over in her hand. They were so solid, it felt almost impossible to even break one in half.

As she did all this, Chino was busy checking out her cute little fingers and hands. And her lips. And those sexy freckles that were sprinkled across her soft sweet face. Her long nails looked freshly manicured. The bills she handed him were all fifties and hundreds, neatly stacked. He folded the wad up and stuffed it into his right pocket.

"What are you cut with?" she asked him, gathering up her dope and putting it all back into a bag.

He laughed at the question. "You hell wit' that mouth of yours, ma. Straight up. I got something fo' dat mouth," he chuckled again. "To answer your question, shorty, I'm black."

She was speechless, but his bronze-like caramel-colored skintone reflected more of a Latino background, one which she was familiar with. The way his words flowed from his lips had her soaking wet.

He stood up and looked down at her. "What are you cut with? And where you from?"

"I'm from the Bronx...BX...NY! I'm all Bo-dee-qua. You didn't see the New York tag on my Mercedes?"

"Oh, Puerto Rican. Naw, I didn't see the tag. I was tryin' to avoid all them cops, so I ain't pay it no attention, ma. Where's your man at?"

46

She frowned, "The fuck if I know. He left me...earlier this morning."

Chino tossed those words around in his head. Damn! I wanna dick this pretty bitch down! he told himself. Then he peeked through the blinds again. There were three detectives walking past his truck parked out in front, one carrying a camera, the other a clipboard. They seemed to be pointing at the burnt rubber left by the tire tracks, then one of them took a photograph of the Honda he'd sideswiped last night.

After taking all this in, he turned around and asked her, "Can I hang out here 'till all these po-leese clear out?"

Alexis didn't respond right away, but the question brought a smile to her face. She hid her bag of crack under a pillow on her loveseat, then sashayed over and stood next to him. She also peered out through the blinds, surprised at the sight of a federal ATF agent wearing a dark-blue flak jacket. He was gathered around a few other officers up the block, a pistol strapped to his leg.

She grabbed hold of one of his hands. "Come on, let's go to my boudoir. Don't worry, you're safe from all them police officers here. All you got to worry about is little ol' me."

Chapter 6

He was sweating hot slugs and horrified when he heard the pup's sudden outburst of barking just outside her bedroom window. Then came a knock at the front door.

TAP! TAP! TAP!

Alexis was all over him like a hungry wildcat, even though he was having a serious problem keeping his dick erect. With a hundred-thousand dollars of ecstasy buy-money hidden in his truck and the feds just outside the door...and up the street...it was difficult to focus on the deep wet pussy that was splashing around and bouncing vigorously on top of him.

KNOCK! KNOCK! KNOCK!

Becoming nervous herself now, Alexis climbed off the bed after dismounting Chino and peeked through the miniblinds. There was a red and white van parked at the curb. "It's the local news—fuck!" she expounded.

Her well-toned arms struggled for a moment, but eventually she was able to lift up the bedroom window. "What is it?" she asked.

An older white man wearing make-up and a perfectly shaped toupee, silver-framed eyeglasses and a colorful tie, tiptoed over closer to the window, careful to stay out of licking range of the thirsty puppy who was whining and yapping at him. And not far away stood another man aiming a video camera at the window.

"Yes ma'am, can we interview you? There was..." he began explaining "five young men were killed, execution-style a few houses down the street, and no one else in the neighborhood is willing to cooperate with me. But I feel this is a very newsworthy story. Will you pl—"

"Tell him no," whispered Chino. "Fuck him!"

"I'm not willing to be interviewed. Get out of my yard wit' that camera!" She slammed down the window and turned toward Chino who was reaching down on the side of the bed for his clothes, hoping to quickly get dressed and bounce. But Alexis pushed him onto his back on the bed and leaped up, straddling his midsection as she gripped his chest, her fingernails sinking in.

Gritting his teeth, he moaned, "Look, ma...ouch! M-my mind ain't on this... sorry. I'm 'posed to be halfway to Chicago by now. My thoughts are on my money. Ya' mean?"

But Alexis didn't need to reply to that comment because the look in her eyes said it all. She commanded total compliance! Once she wiggled around for a few seconds and raised her hips, his wrinkled limp dick began to slowly rise up and even without the use of her hands she was able to reinsert his obedient rod back deep inside her eager womb. There was nothing Alexis wanted that she couldn't get...one way or another!

So, for the next hour nothing else in the entire world mattered or existed except for the pain and pleasure Chino and Alexis shared on her very expensive and quite damp queen-sized sheets.It was during this heated coupling that a hot and sweat-dripping union was formed and the relationship cemented.

*****

The expression on her face revealed a sense of worry and fear, Danny thought to himself as Uncle Harold introduced him to Lucy. She was a wiry 36-pound well-conditioned and muscular buckskin-colored pit bull with a huge square-shaped head and bulging black eyeballs. She was pacing back and forth in her cage, tongue dangling, like she was preparing her mind for something important.

Just then Harold disturbed Danny's futile attempt at reading Lucy's mind. "C'mon, boy, let me show you the rest of the farm."

Danny was in awe of his surroundings, completely overwhelmed with what he saw, a seemingly "pit bull paradise" way out here in the boondocks. There was dog kennel after dog kennel stretching out the length of a football field, all neatly lined up with a single pit bull in each cage. They were all different colors and sizes, with one nearby kennel having seven or eight small spotted puppies inside, all play-wrestling and having a ball.

Harold had six employees who were wearing black and blue matching uniforms, most of them busy cleaning cages. On the back of their polo-style shirts was imprinted Cold-Blooded Kennels. The men worked with what appeared to be a never-ending rhythm and seemed to take much pride in their jobs. They constantly talked to the dogs, calling them by their names. As Danny watched, he got the impression that they all looked like crack smokers, which was a good observation.

He was standing beside his uncle who was taking an incoming call on his cell phone, trying desperately to find a spot to stand where he could get a decent reception.

"Dammit! Okay, I can hear you now...yeah, we got Lucy on deck t'night...fifty large on the line...should be a big turnout..."

Danny listened while Harold gave out directions to his compound, at the same time his eyes taking in the huge red and white barn where a couple of the workers led a charcoal-colored, low-to-the-grind thick massive-sized pit bull on a heavy duty-lookin chain. From where he was standing, Danny could see them as they put the pit up on a treadmill that was just one of many along a wall. The dog began...

"Yeah, nephew, we got a show t'night. Now, you just keep an eye on e'erbody. You'll be like my undercover security. I'll give you a uniform, radio...you know, a walkie-talkie. Just make yo' rounds, make sho nobody fuckin' 'round wit' the dogs in this area," he motioned with both arms before continuing on. "Make sho ain't no muthafuckas breakin' in cars. It'll be a big show t'night, you'll see, nephew. Now, c'mon, let me introduce you to the guys. You do good, I'ma have you supervising 'em." He smiled at his nephew, laying a very large and heavy hand on Danny's shoulder, a larger burden on his mind.

Later, after placing the black pistol that once belonged to Sugar Man under the mattress, Danny dumped out all of his clothes onto the small twin-sized bed. The rubberband-bounded stacks of cash spilled out, followed by the large clear bags of dope. He quickly pulled open one of the bags and removed an ounce of weed, setting it aside, then peeled off a thin stack of hundreds and put it in his pocket before stashing the rest of the money and drugs in a small closet.

When he peered inside the closet, he noticed so many cobwebs hanging in it that he decided to sweep it out. The room was tiny as hell, but it had a color TV sittin' on a dresser that also had a matching nightstand.

A single window overlooked the unique pit bull farm and he could see three other buildings that were within eyesight, similar to his living quarters. There was no carpeting in his room, just old unstained wooden floors. But it was certainly better than a jail cell, he considered as he swept up a pile of dirt with a broom.

He was yawning now as he sat on the porch, observing the scene before him. Trucks and cars by the dozen began pulling into the complex, even a sweet-looking candy-painted H2 Hummer rolling on in. Danny was scratching his head as he watched, wishing he had something in which to roll his weed. The scent of burning marijuana soon permeated the country air, followed by the aroma of meat frying on a grill. He was hungry and getting sleepy while many of the out-of-towners were busy setting up tents and small barbecue grills, all of which was exciting to him.

Just about then he glanced over and noticed a young yellow-bone girl with long black hair sitting on a folding chair with a laptop computer resting on her legs. She was sitting next to a sleek-looking 40-foot silver and black RV with Ohio license plates. Hanging from the side of the RV was a huge matching banner which read SHUT 'EM DOWN KENNELS. Danny guessed her to be about 17 or 18 years old at the most as he admired her Coke bottle-like figure. She winked at him, then smiled and giggled.

The crowd was swelling in size by the hour as the sun began falling. The small refrigerator in his sleeping shack was empty except for a single can of Budweiser, and Harold was nowhere to be found, so Danny was sort of forced to go mingle in the crowd, his hunger was so intense. He finally came upon one of Harold's employees standing over what appeared to be a blackened 55-gallon steel barrel that had been cut in half and converted into a barbecue grill. He had an array of different kinds of meat sizzling on top. The man was an older bald-headed brown-skinned guy, possibly in his fifties. Music was playing from a nearby radio, some old classic song, and Danny just stood there staring at the smoke rising up toward the sky as it poured from the grill.

"Youngsta, ya hungry?"

"Yeah, I'm starvin'. I ain't ate shit all day."

The hardworking man prodded and poked at the tender meat with a long wooden handle fork, then pulled off a thick greasy hamburger and a sausage from the grill and laid them on a paper plate. "Bobbycue sauce an' buns ova dere," he mumbled, pointing at a folding table.

After wolfing down and enjoying the burger and sausage, Danny handed the old man a crisp hundred-dollar bill, causing his eyes to light up. He snatched it!

"What dis fo'? Dis bobbycue free."

"That's yours, ol' school," he told him. "What's your name?"

"Cecile...yours?"

"Danny."

"Well, I 'preciate the tip, youngsta. Don't get many of dem dese days."

"You will. I'm livin' here now. I got some of that dope, too, but right now I need a cigar to roll a blunt wit'. Can you find me a couple?"

Cecile started pulling some of the meat off the fire and said, "Gimme a minute. Cecile'll fin' you some blunts. Maybe later you'll let Cecile sample some of that hardball."

"Yeah, I got you, ol' school. It's...one guy said it wasn't that good."

"I'll be da judge of dat. Prob'ly just need recooking, yep," Cecile explained, offering Danny a friendly smile afterwards.

*****

Inside the custom-designed barn the crowd was cheering for more action, it was the final match of the night and the 12' x 12' tan carpeting inside the box was gory looking with a lot of blood and piss. The awful stench of dog shit permeated the warm air like a fine mist and it stunk like a slaughterhouse. Flies were everywhere.

Danny had never known such a savage bloodsport even existed. There was row upon row of bleachers for standing-only spectators, people placing bets on their favorite dogs, lots of drinking and smoking and laughing. These were mostly high rollers and true dog men. Some guys event brought their girlfriends to enjoy the gruesome matches.

Meanwhile, Lucy's opponent was an all white bitch named Tina Marie, a young nasty looking three-time champion. Danny had overheard a group of Puerto Ricans saying she was off of "Mayday and Red Boy Jocko" bloodlines. He'd never heard of that before. The dog seemed to be crying like it pained her to no end to be the last fighter of the evening's festivities. She'd witnessed the fate of so many sporting dogs before her in past fights. As her handler carried her into the enclosure by climbing over the short wall encircling the pit, Tina Marie was looking all around for her opponent. After she'd been washed and scrubbed, she weighed in right at 35 pounds even. Her protruding jaws appeared strong enough to snap steel in half as her Spanish speaking handler whispered sweet words in her ears while massaging her muscular burly-like chest.

Back in a dark corner of the barn, near the front entrance, Danny fired up another blunt after witnessing the execution of dogs who'd lost earlier matches by getting shot in the head. The way that white smoke arose from the entry wound caused by the bullet was fucking him up, so when someone behind him asked softly, "What's your name?" he nearly jumped out of his skin! He turned around and saw that cute young girl from Ohio smiling at him. She reached out her hand indicating that she wanted to hit his exotic-smelling blunt. She was wearing a sexy eye-catching sundress. When he passed it to her, she wrapped her juicy red lips around the blunt. She hit it.

Uncle Harold was shirtless and all greased up as he carried Lucy to her corner of the pit. But you could barely see the dog, except for her paws dangling at his side, because he was so incredibly wide across his back.

Both of the bitches were angry now, wanting nothing more than to end this battle as quickly as possible. They were sizing up each other, sniffing while looking for any sign of weakness, neither one finding any. They had both been bred and trained explicitly for this gruesome sport, to be killers, which is exactly what they came here tonight to do. Some of the spectators had come from as far away as England to witness this evil event first hand.

With fifty-thousand of his own money riding on Lucy, and another five or ten grand in side bets already locked in, Harold was intense as he squatted down in his corner of the box while clutching the dog beneath her chest. He and Lucy, skin to skin soul to soul. And he could feel her heart pounding in harmony with his own heart just the way he liked to. Harold always believed that his own freak-like size intimidated the opponent's dog as well as the dog's handler.

Not this night!

Standing in the center of the box, a tall thin referee with a grey beard crouched down to look both dog handlers square in the eye, one at a time. "Face your dogs!" he shouted, then took three or four steps backwards as he cleared the floor before raising his long arms in the air and adding, "Release your dogs!"

With their mouths wide open and razor-sharp fangs bared, both beasts attacked, nose-diving into each other. The powerful head-on collision sounded like an explosion! Blood splattered all across the two-foot-high walls surrounding the box and the crowd went berserk. Lucy quickly grabbed hold of the other dog with a tight suffocating grip around its neck. She furiously yanked and slung Tina Marie from side to side, crashing her into a corner with enough impact to crack one of the panels in the wooden box.

"Get my money, Lucy! Don't let 'er go! Kill 'er, girl...kill 'er!" hollered Harold.

Lucy's strong wide rear-legged stance kept her in total control, clearly dominating the other dog as she worked her strangulation hold deeper and deeper. Now on her back, the only thing Tina Marie could do was worm and wiggle, all to no avail. She tried futilely to push her violent opponent off of her, using her hind legs, but simply couldn't fend off Lucy's death grip. Her lungs were near empty when she suddenly flipped over and pulled away, causing both killer dogs to become entangled with each other. Blood from Tina Marie was dripping from Lucy's flesh-shredding mouth. All at once Tina Marie's face-game took a hold and she recoiled for a split second, then counter-attacked, taking a couple quick bone-shattering chomps at Lucy's nose. It was a risky move, but the second bite she took clamped down so painfully tight on Lucy's nose that she screamed and tried to back away. But Tina out-muscled her, overpowering her and crushing her against the side of the wall, then ripped her nose completely off.

Next she went for the throat!

They'd now been grappling for nearly ten minutes, both angling and veering while brawling, each of them hell bent on taking the other's last breath from them. They were slinging flesh and fur, purple-red blood squirting from near fatal open wounds while both handlers were hunkered down in their respective corners coaching their dogs, screaming at the top of their lungs right along with the crowd.

Lucy had been on the bottom of the vicious altercation for the past few minutes, getting shaken repulsively and being out-maneuvered while on the brink of bleeding out from a torn artery that had been exposed and was now pulsating in her hind leg. And she was leaking bad!

"Lucy...c' mon, girl...get right, girl! Don't g-give up!" cried Harold as he pulled a snot rag from his pants pocket and wiped his dark perspiring face.

*****

The interior of the tricked-out RV was very nice. It resembled the inside of an expensive home, thought Danny, just as he was about to reach his peak. He thrust forward two more times, then cried out, "Ohhh...yes, Monica. Your pussy's so good and tight!"

He had been lying there on top of her for the past few minutes, both of them trying to catch their breath, when suddenly they heard, "Where the fuck you at, nigga?" It had come crackling through the walkie-talkie that was setting on the floor of the RV right next to Danny's pants.

"Shit! It's my uncle, Monica...I got to go!"

"I'm goin' with you," she replied, quickly slipping back into her cute sundress.

They were holding hands as then entered the barn, trying to avoid the crowd of people. Some were stopping to pay off their bets in cash while others were simply talking and arguing about the matches they'd just witnessed.

"That's my dad's dog," whispered Monica, pointing a finger at Tina Marie. Kneeling next to the dog was a Spanish-looking guy who was injecting a long needle into her side. Then he sponged off her head and the rest of her body before carefully stitching up a long disgusting looking gash under her neck. Another guy came over carrying a portable metal kennel and set it down next to the now four-time champion, Tina Marie. The dog had a certain twinkle in her eyes as she scanned her surroundings.

"Look at this dumb nigger!" yelled Tina Marie's handler as he stood up.

Harol was standing there, his eyes tearing up, still in the box and holding an aluminum baseball bat in his right hand. Lucy had just staggered over and collapsed at his feet, her eyes looking up at him but not able to see. She was completely blind. Then, with all his strength and hulking might, Harold raised the bat up above his head and came down with a crushing blow to Lucy's head, pummeling and pulverizing her with the bat again and again and again...and once more. He kept smashing the poor dog's head until squishy-looking pink brain matter oozed from her mouth, her eye sockets and her ears. Harold was covered with blood, and Lucy was dead game. A few sickened onlookers captured his unsportsman like rage with their cell phones.

After discarding the bat, he wrinkled his flaring nostrils and turned his wandering red eyeballs on Danny, who fearful wrestled his sweaty hand free from the young girl.

Chapter 7

While sitting at the bar in an upscale nightclub, Becky was feeling too good off the pills she had popped. All she kept thinking about was the conversation she overheard Chino and Kilo having earlier that morning.

That's sweet of Chino to want me to go back to law school, but I'm done living an uneventful life, she thought before throwing back a double shot of Seagram's Gin. "School or no school, guys are going to learn to value my worth," she frowned. Becky kind of figured Chino was going to double back for Alexis, so when he saw his truck parked outside her house she knew he was fucking her. And that's what led her to the bar tonight.

When Jahiem's 'Put That Woman First' came on Becky jumped up, swaying her hips, while singing drunkenly. It had been so long since Chino had made love to her that now she just craved a soft touch, so when the caramel brown-skinned sista started dancing with her she enjoyed it to the max.

Looking into her slanted hazel eyes, and feeling the heat exuding from her voluptuous ass grinding against her caused Becky to get moist between her thighs. "I'm Becky," she screamed over the music.

"Deeiaz," the goddess responded with.

As they continued grinding on each other for the next three songs, a man approached them. When Becky laid eyes on his six-foot-one-inch frame, with his dreads pulled back, she started having a slight orgasm.

"Bella it's time for us to move around," the man commanded with his hand out, waiting for Deeiaz to take it. She did.

"Okay. Well, Becky, it was nice meeting and feeling you." While letting her dreads down, she gave her a mystical lioness look.

"Same here. I wish we could do this again, but I see you're taken," Becky said, watching the guy wrap his arm around her waist in a protective lover way. Seeing that reminded her of how Chino use to be.

"Oh, where's my manners. Becky this is De'Audie." She smiled, "King, this is Becky. And to answer your question: we always let sexy people into our affairs." With that, she handed her a business card and the couple headed for the exit of the club.

*****

Pacing back and forth, Olivia was uncertain about how she was going to play it. She knew CC's death was revenge behind Danny's actions, yet now she felt she had to retaliate for both her losses. It all started with some bad work. she thought. But that's the chances you take in the dope game. She shook her head, and dialed Alexis' number. "Hey, Lex."

"What's up? Olivia...uh, mmmmm. What you doin'?

"I was about to say I'm on my way over to talk about us getting straight but it sounds like you busy." Olivia could hear soft moaning, as Alexis began giggling and said, "Stop boy!"

"I'm never too busy to talk about getting right, come over. I'm here."

With that, she hung up and hopped in her Seville, and merged into traffic. Even though her life was one of the ghetto lavished, she missed the days when things were simple. She reached into her Berkin bag for a Vicodin, then popped one. As she pulled up to Alexis' house she saw a light-skinned dude leaving while Alexis was still at the front door smiling with this 'I just got fucked so good' glow.

Smiling, while walking into the house, Olivia said, "I want all the details, with yo' freaky ass."

"Girl, that and a blunt of this purple he left, coming right up."

Olivia sat down noticing the colorful pills sitting on the end table. "Lex, what are these?" She picked up a few to examine.

"Oh, them" she said, "Those are X-pills. This girl, umm, Becky left. I was gone try 'em but she pulled a bag of them out her pussy, so I said I'm good."

Laughing at Alexis' comment and facial expressions, she said, "That's how a bitch gotta traffic. Plus you can steal shit and a mothafucka would never know unless they hip."

"Oh yeah. And how is you so hip? Let me find out you been traffickin'."

"Honey please. Huh, let's try 'em and get down to what I came here for."

"Alright..." she replied, firing up the weed. She walked into the kitchen, returning with two bottled waters. She handed Olivia one.

After they popped the ecstasy pills, Olivia started her spiel about how they needed to find a new plug. They cried about the loss of CC, and tried to make sense of the circumstances, too. When suddenly they started getting hot, and full of sexual energy. Looking at Alexis you would've thought she was coked up by the way her pupils were dilated.

Olivia said, "Bitch! I'm soooo high! We need some music and drinks."

The high Olivia got off the Vicodins was a cool chill one, but this one was a real rush, and she loved it!

Chapter 8

Chino had just gotten off the phone with Kilo, telling him to drop some work off on the soldiers in the trenches. Even though he was on, he still had his eyes open for his next lick. Like a dog searching for a bone, he was searching for prey.

Getting a text from Becky he ignored it, he didn't have time to baby her, he was on a money hunt. The trip to and from Chicago had turned out well. Inside, Chino was patting himself on the back, pulling his truck into the stash house driveway. His thoughts turned to Alexis, as he compared her to Becky. As he sat there in his truck he could hear his pit bull in the back of the house barking. Getting inside, Chino called for him, causing the dog to scratch at the door.

"What's up Four? Daddy's man miss him?" he asked, letting the 60 pound tiger striped brindle pit bull out. Running through the house was his usual program, so that's what he did.

It had been a few days since Chino and Kilo had smoked them Crips, and got them for the work he had served them. Not thinking of a nigga trying to get at him, he didn't panic about the knock at the door.

"Who is it? Who you?"

Still not getting an answer, he went to look at the surveillance monitor mounted up over the fireplace, but before he could, the front door came crashing down. Seeing two masked men, Chino darted towards the back door.

Boom! Boom! Boom!

As three shotgun blasts volleyed holes in the wall in front of him, Chino nose-dove into the back bedroom. Rolling over onto his back he pulled out his P89. That's when one of the intruders broke out into a high-pitched scream! Four was locked on to the back of dude's thigh, shaking, pulling, shaking, doing his damn best at protecting his master.

"Shit! Ahhhhhhhh! Shoot this mufucka, bruh!!"

With that small window of opportunity, Chino took control of the home-invasion, firing five rounds into the other one's chest. As Four was trying to rip the dude a new hole, Chino rose to his feet, noticing blood splattered all across the white walls. The man was crying out for help! Snatching the ski mask off the guy, Chino asked, "Who sent y'all?"

"Fuck you pussy!" he spat. "Your days numbered!" He spit a glob of mucus in Chino's face, showing his teeth as he endured the agonizing pain Four was still inflicting with pleasure.

"Yeah, but yours is already up. On Chief, pussy!"

Boc! Boc! Boc!

Three shots sent his body crashing into the wall where he slid down it. As he did this, Four made a complete mess of his face by removing it.

*****

Alexis had been sprung off the ecstasy ever since the first day she'd tried them. On this morning, she'd woke up in a cold shivering sweat, as she explained this to Chino over the phone.

"What you been using, ma?" he asked her.

"Just them pills Becky left here."

"Oh yeah," he replied. "When was the last time you was rollin'?"

"Umm, like three days ago. I ain't got no more."

"I'm on my way over," Chino said.

"I'm going to get in the shower. I'll be waiting for you. I hope you got some skittles for me. I'm trying to feel the rainbow."

"Hey, you ain't know, I'm the skittle king," bragged Chino.

After a couple hot sessions of fucking, Chino left Alexis' house and got off in traffic, chasing his next dollar.

*****

Now, Alexis found every day of her life filled with never-ending sex and ecstasy parties. Today was no different. After getting her makeup together, she slid into a new Versace miniskirt, and Louis Vuitton pumps. Looking in the mirror making sure her pretty girl swag was on fleek, she rested a pair of sexy 24K gold Ferragamo eyeglasses on her face. After that, it was off to the club.

She was not standing in line but a few minutes when a dude walked up on her offering to pay her way inside. She looked up seeing the Cuban's complexion was dark like a Haitian, and handsome. Smiling, showing off her pearly whites, they made their way inside the packed night spot.

He greeted her with, "I'm Stephon."

67

Before she replied, she had to find her way back to the moment because she was lost in his laid back, GQ persona. He was killing it with some all white Balmain, a Louis belt, and a silk Versace button up. With his icy big-face Rolex, you knew papi was playing with a large bag.

"I'm Alexis. How come this my first time ever seeing you here?" she asked as they sat in VIP. She had become a known regular at the club.

"I'm not too much of a party-goer. I'm into counting Benjamins. That's what makes me happy."

She was really feeling him, like his swag was on 101. He smelled so good, his conversation was versatile, plus he was about his paper, and his big dick print was mouthwatering to her. All she could think about was locking him down.

"So I'm like ready to leave! What's up?"

"Oh, okay well," he began saying, his phone ringing. "I got to go myself. So I guess I will be walking you to your car." He smiled.

As Alexis heard those words she was pissed that she couldn't get a look at Mr. Handsome naked tonight. Stephon had told her he worked for his uncle, named Bull, who owned a concrete company. Initially she was willing to believe him, but this call at midnight said otherwise.

When they got to her Benz in the club's parking lot, she caught him nodding his approval while looking down at her ass. Trading numbers, he walked over to his Lexus, and meanwhile, she saved his number under 'New Boo'.

*****

Danny was fed up with getting Alexis' voicemail. When Olivia confirmed it, that she had a new nigga, he said, "fuck her." Now he filled his days with working out, and studying the many different varieties of game dogs. It was amazing, certain bloodlines fought harder than others, while some fought smarter. And some, they didn't fight at all, those dogs were always executed.

On this night, Monica had caught a Greyhound bus down from Ohio, and Danny had a taxi cab bring her to his living quarters. He was jacked out of his mind off the ecstasy, and couldn't wait to try all the freaky things Alexis had taught him on Monica. Her pussy was tighter anyway. He couldn't wait to eat it. They'd been talking on the phone about her spending a couple weeks with him. Uncle Harold's compound was so huge, he wouldn't even know she was there. Nor would he care.

"Oh Goddd! Fuck me. Yes Danny!" hissed Monica, looking back over her shoulder as he drilled her doggy-style. "Shhhitt! I'm cum-m-ming!" she screamed while thrusting her ass back and clenching the covers.

Danny had been long stroking her for 45-minutes straight, and for the first time in her life she felt the magic of multiple orgasms. "Fuck! M-meeee, damnit, you fuckin' this pussy so damn good. I'm cumming again!"

Like a dog, Danny growled, then barked, standing up in the pussy, pounding his dick deeper into her cervix, reaching her G-Spot with ease as she exploded again, for the third time! Her pussy was sloppy wet, literally soaked, making all kinds of squishy sounds. He felt his balls tingle as her vaginal muscles contracted tightly in spasms. "Yeah, yeah, oh, mmm, shit!" he cried snatching his swipe out, shooting his jism all over her round ass cheeks.

"Damn bae, you wore me out. Come on let's cuddle for a second," Monica cooed. Her center was still thumping, she could feel it pulsating inside her womb. Her nipples were so hard till she rubbed one, soon feeling Danny's arms wrapping around her. The room was dark and cozy, and hot as hell. After reaching for a glass of water and drinking it, Danny asked, "When your dad's grand champion mates, can I get one of them pups?" He was still missing his pup back in St. Louis. Even though Uncle Harold said he was going to give him a puppy; after the unforgettable comeback Tina Marie had made, he figured he'd get that bloodline.

"Okay. But we've also got a big black nasty monster they call Forbidden. A male. He's young, but he's mine."

"Are y'all gonna mate it with Tina Marie?"

"Naw, my pops don't cross breed. But I'm thinking about starting my own kennel. I just need a good bitch. What you think?" she asked rolling on top of him.

"Shid, that's what's up. If that's what you want, then I'll help you. We can get on the computer and look around," he suggested.

Cracking a smile prettier than a diamond, she leaned over him and kissed his forehead, then his lips. "Thanks babe." She smiled, kissing a trail across his chest, down his abs, straight to his love pipe. She filled her mouth with it. Taking him completely into her throat without gagging.

70

*****

As Kilo knifed through late-night traffic, dropping off dope and picking up cash, he was still thinking about Chino. In fact, he was furious someone attempted to take his life.

"Damn, niggas really tried to get at cha," he mumbled to no one at all. He was trying to figure out who sent them, and could it have been vengeance for their most recent lick. As he dropped off a four-way and 500 pills to one of the guys, Kilo spotted Becky in her Jeep driving by in the opposite direction. His mind got to wondering. Even though he always wanted to fuck Becky, he wasn't cool with the thought of her setting him or Chino up.

"Let me find out that was yo' work, it's gone be a great day in hell," he stated. He licked his lips as he watched her bend the corner near some projects.

At the same time Chino was chilling with his main girl, Melissa, smoking a joint of Kat Piss, thinking about the same thing. Becky had been on some distant shit lately, and the other day she tripped out about who he was fucking. Which was the main reason he was here with Melissa now.

"Baby, you want something out the kitchen?" Melissa asked.

"Yeah, make me a fried turkey ham and cheese sandwich."

"Okay, boo," she said, giving him a full show of her ass cheeks hanging from her boy shorts.

Getting a text from Alexis, Chino started chuckling. He was really becoming fond of her, and her hustling ambition was an even more plus.

"When can I get back up with you, because my girl ran out on me?" she texted, meaning: she needed more coke.

71

He texted back with, "give me 45 mins, I'll be around to make sure she get right."

Walking into the kitchen, Chino got the perfect view as Melissa bent over inside the refrigerator. He palmed her ass, she smiled, then kissed him. Even though Melissa was urban model material, and a church-going type of girl, with a good job, Chino couldn't get enough of his new sex addict, Alexis.

"Aye bae, I got to shoot a move."

Poking out her bottom lip, she said, "What about your sandwich?" She sat the plate down on the counter top and put her hands on her hips.

"I'm cool. Come lock this door and give me some love."

While walking him to the front door, she guided her tongue down his throat, feeling his strong hands gripping her ass. After locking the door, Melissa rushed to her phone to put her own "move" in motion.

Chapter 9

As Alexis and Olivia were bagging up their coke, they were both in deep thought. Using a small spoon and a digital scale, they were putting 8 grams of cut on every 20 grams of raw.

Olivia was trying to figure out why Danny was so concerned about Alexis. While Alexis was thinking about Stephon, and Chino. Even though Chino was super fly and plugged, she didn't see a long life with him. Not like how she saw with Stephon.

"Bitch, we need to find a way to get our powder clientele up," stated Olivia. She began counting all the ounces she'd bagged up in sandwich baggies.

"Yeah, I know that's right. And Chino on some different shit now, too."

"Like what?" asked Olivia, firing up a cigarette.

"Well, he said he 'bout to get out the coke game and deal with the ecstasy pills, exclusively for a while."

"What? That nigga trippin'...so what, now we need a new plug. It's always something!"

Olivia pulled hard on her Newport, frustrated, exhaling smoke; not knowing Alexis was already 10 steps ahead of her with getting a new supplier. And just before explaining her plans the front door came crashing wide open!

"DEA! Freeze! Nobody move!"

"ATF, we have a ... search warrant!" a gun-pointing agent yelled.

As Alexis saw the officers rushing inside she jumped up, scrambling to the bathroom in a desperate attempt to flush the work. Not even making it to the hallway before she was tackled to the carpet and handcuffed.

"Bitch, I said don't move!" The agent backhanded her across the face.

*****

This was about to be the first fight Danny would be betting on, and when he looked at Forbidden, he knew this was money in the bag. Forbidden was in excellent fighting shape. He was ripped up and unusually calm. His dark eyesballs were locked-in on whatever it was he was seeing in his boulder-shaped head. His opponent barking in the distance didn't faze him, neither did the noise level that was growing louder for the start of this event. Both dogs having been bathed and weighed in, it was now time for battle in this small town in Decatur, Illinois.

Dog men were placing their bets in a frenzy. That's when Monica ran up, "Hey babe, do you wanna release Forbidden?" she asked.

"Hell yeah!" He put his diamond chain around Monica's neck and took his shirt off.

After the ref was done checking the beasts, Danny hugged Forbidden like uncle would always do before a match. He felt himself almost become one with the dog, as Forbidden licked his lips at the sight of his contender. "Watch that dog boy boy. Kill dat dog for Daddy." The more he sweet talked to Forbidden, the more he zoned out. His jaw muscles looked like two crushing machines, having been developed by tugging and biting car tires since birth.

The ref yelled, "Is you ready?" then he said it again. Then he yelled "Scratch!" With that, both animals were released, and the show was on!

Being the chest-hitter he was, Forbidden attacked low, seeking instant leverage by driving his enemy backwards. The other hound defended the lower assault by clamping onto his head. While Forbidden's fangs were slicing holes into his chest. As Forbidden did a crowd-pleasing 40-second death-shake, both dogs crashed into the wooden box. Forbidden used the power of his hind legs to drive his opponent upwards, and off balance.

"Let's go! Come on Forbidden! Go for the neck!" coached Danny. As if he'd been trained by Danny on command, Forbidden released and shot for the neck. The other dog dodged the unexpected lunging move and countered by locking onto Forbidden's paw, grinding its mighty teeth on bone, aiming to shatter it. And damn near doing so!

"Break that leg Tazz! Come on my nigga...squeeze!" yelled the dog's corner. "Rip it off!"

After both animals spun in a circle, entwined, Forbidden found a weakness and exploited it! With his fangs clamping down on the back of Tazz's neck, skillfully, Forbidden shook him around the box for the next 30 seconds, dominating the match. It was nasty, foam, blood, shit and slob slung everywhere! Tazz's cry for help must've touched his owner's heart, "Let me get a gotdamn re-scratch!" yelled dude with a defeated voice, exuding pain and embarrassment.

With a wooden breaking stick rammed into Forbidden's mouth, down into his throat, Danny unlocked his mighty grip from around the other dog. Although Forbidden was limping a bit he pleaded to finish what he started here. You could see it in his eyes. He wanted nothing short of killing the other beast. His tail stood straight out, eager for more action. He whined for it. After the ref yelled out some house rules that Forbidden wasn't trying to hear, when he said "Ready...ready, scratch!" Forbidden shot out like a sniper's bullet! He locked back on to Tazz, flipping him over onto his back, mauling his throat, tearing his chest apart! "That's it! That's the fight!" yelled the ref, motioning for Danny to restrain his animal. Tazz laid there, bleeding out, crying, his muscles twitching, panting for air, death hovered above him.

Danny was geeked, he won his first match, plus doubled the four grand he'd bet. Monica was all smiles. She kissed Forbidden's nose. Monica's uncle then took Forbidden from Danny and began to gently stitch up a terrible gash on his foot, and toweled him off. He watched closely, as the man inserted a small IV drip into the inner thigh of his champion in order to rehydrate his dog as quickly as possible. "You did good," the Spanish man told Danny. "Forbidden like to be coached in English. He's not bilingual just yet." He smiled.

76

Danny's phone rang as he observed the post-fight care Forbidden was now receiving. "Hello," he answered, "whud up, Unc?"

"Man nephew, yo' aunt Olivia and Alexis locked up."

*****

It had been over a week since Becky had gotten Deeiaz's number. She wasn't really into women, but the way Deeiaz caressed her body had her curious and second guessing. Not to forget, the dude she was with was attractive. The thought of them had her hot.

"So what should we do?" Becky asker her poodle, named Lovely. "Call or wait?"

With a high-pitched "Arf!" Becky smiled at her reply and said, "Yeah, I think I should call, too."

After another "Yip!" Becky was off and running, dialing the number.

"Hello."

When Becky heard the deep smooth male's voice she froze up, thinking she had the wrong number until she heard the voice again, and her pussy twitched like it never did before.

"Umm, is Deeiaz around?" she asked in a shy seductive way.

"And whom I speaking with?"

"Becky."

"Becky," he said, "hello, Becky." There was a pause. "Becky, it's so good to finally hear from you. You had me thinking you wasn't interested."

"Oh nawl, it's nothing like that. I was just so busy." For the next half an hour they got better acquainted. She spoke with Deeiaz, and they exchanged photos and laughs. They were really vibing with one another when Deeiaz finally said, "Okay Becky, I'll call you later."

"All right. Be safe. Call me..."

Becky was feeling Deeiaz, her voice was sweet, and commanding. You know, the kind of commands you long to get.

Then she sat there thinking about their lingerie line 'Succulent', and how they travel all over the world. Deeiaz had texted her pictures of the bras, panties, garter belts, and things. And she wanted to ask her did she really think she had what it took. Becky recalled those eyes of Deeiaz's, they were the eyes of a cold-hearted woman. *Succulent lingerie...not with those eyes*, Becky thought. *There's more to this fashion story*. Just then the thought of Paris, came to mind, Deeiaz had said, *"The world is ours."* And Becky wanted to be a part of that world. All her life she'd been told she was gorgeous. But she thought she was fat. She walked to a full-length mirror in her bedroom, looked at her curvy 48 inches of pure natural ass and hips, turning around. She smiled at what she saw, and popped a couple blue dolphins afterwards.

Chapter 10

"You ready my G?" Chino asked Kilo.

"Hell yeah, let's get paid, my nigga."

As they climbed out of Kilo's old school Chevy, perched on some 3-piece Forgiatos, they were ready to make a switch in their operation.

Chino had met this cat called Audie who assured him that he could help him with his dilemma. They had met at a rave party in St. Louis. Chino had observed dude hand off two Ziploc bags to a sexy Latina, who in turn walked them over to some guys across the dance floor.

Without fear, Chino made his way towards Audie, but got stopped some 10 to 12 feet away by a Haitian and Brazilian chick, both holding sub-compact M-14s.

"What cha want?" asked Audie, waving his pistol at Chino.

"I was just tryin' to talk a little business."

"I have no business with cha. So what is it cha want?"

With confidence Chino explained, "And in my eyes that's a bad thing. Because I can be beneficial to you."

Puffing on his cigar stuffed with a blend of Purple Haze and Sour Diesel, Audie began sizing Chino up. After a moment of calculating, he finally welcomed him over to his table.

"So, what's your name, and what business can you help me with?" asked Audie, passing Chino the blunt.

After a hard pull on the blunt, Chino began coughing. He handed the blunt back. Next, he made eye contact and spit his game, which led him to the huge ranch-style home him and Kilo was at now.

Once they were patted down during a routine weapons check, they were escorted to Audie. Walking inside the well-furnished room, Chino peeped the German Rottweiler in one corner, and a sable-colored Shepard in another. Audie was seated with one leg across the other.

"It's good to see you," Audie said.

"Vice-versa. So, tell me something good?" Chino was ready to get to them pills and flood the streets of the Midwest. Audie was clearly much bigger than his Chicago connect, but Chino sensed Audie had a different objective in mind. An ulterior motive. He could feel it.

"Yes, something good," he began by looking over at a much thicker Suki Waterhouse look-alike wearing a black maid's outfit. "Sabrina please bring us a bottle of 1738 and a Dutch," said Audie. She returned shortly with the bottle and a pre-stuffed Dutch. Audie then began to speak his mind. "Okay, I understand that you, and your friend want to get riches, and I respect that. But in dealing with me it's more on the lines of a lifetime thing, a relationship."

Not saying a word, Chino just stared at him. Yet what Audie didn't know was Chino had been all-in since the age of 9. Seeing that Chino never broke eye contact, he continued. "Now I'm going to give you 300 jars at a time to start. I want all my fuckin' money. No shorts. If you need me, I'm here, but other than that, I expect loyalty before royalty."

Looking at each other with approval, Chino said, "We agree to the terms."

Audie simply stood up, "Okay, with this understanding, Sabrina, bring the girls and some skittles. It's time to party."

*****

As Alexis sat in her jail cell, she was wondering about what was going to happen. She was being charged with conspiracy to distribute cocaine, and distribution of a controlled substance. ATF also found her .22 underneath her mattress. Since this was her first case, her lawyer told her the United States Sentencing Guidelines called for about 5 years, plus another consecutive 5 for the gun. But if she was willing to plead guilty within 48 hours he could get her 5 years total. And if she was also willing to cooperate as an informer, she could get as little as a year...or much less.

The thought of turning into a snitch wasn't an option, she thought. Losing everything she'd gained in the dope game was a painful reality. But what hurt more was losing her freedom for so long. She knew she could do the time, but she was wondering who would be there for her, emotionally.

Leaving out her cell, she went and jumped on the phone. As she stood there, dialing number after number, she got no answer. "What the fuck! So can't nobody answer they phone?!" Alexis was feeling the strain and pain that comes with incarceration.

"It's okay, boo-boo, when Sara stop sucking and bouncing on that dick he'll answer." Snapping her head around to see who made the rude comment, she noticed a dark-chocolate complexioned sister. She was about five-five and said her name was "Sassy." And she lived up to the name too. Ignoring her, she tried Stephon's number since nobody else answered, not even her mother or aunt.

"Hello...you have a collect call from Alexis Sims, an inmate at a federal correctional facility. Press '5' to accept the call or press '7' to block any calls of this nature."

"Hello."

Hearing his voice her heart fluttered and a beautiful smile separated across her face.

"Hey Stephon. I'm so happy you answered, what you doing?"

"I'm glad you did call. What are you in the feds for?"

"Huhhh. Well, the feds raided my house and found some...coke, a pistola, money. They locked me and my friend up. I got denied a bond."

"Oh, damn shorty. What they talkin' about givin' you?" he asked, sincerely concerned.

"Well, they offering me a cop-out for 60 months, or go to trial and risk 25 years, which is my max."

When Stephon got quiet, she thought he hung up, so after she said, "Hello" twice, he answered.

"What's up?"

"I thought you hung up, you alright?" she asked.

"Yeah. Look, what's your name and info so I can write you. And send me a visitation form. I wanna see you, and send you some bread."

Hearing them words, she rattled off her complete info, as he wrote it down.

"Alright, I got it. Look, I'ma be there for you this whole ride. Now—"

"Thank you so much," Alexis said cutting him off, abruptly.

"But, if you plan on tellin', or any shit like that then I'm not doing shit for you."

In Alexis's mind, if that's all it took then the deal was sealed. She had been in the game and knew the rules to snitching. "If you snitch, you die." But one thing that ticked at her mind was why. Why was Stephon trying to do this for her. So she asked him.

"Listen Boo," he replied, "I've been behind them bars myself for a long time. And as a real nigga, and a real man, I got to help my sistas when I can."

Listening to Stephon's tender words caused a lonely tear to roam down her cheek.

Beep-Beep...

"Umm, Okay, well, the phone's about to hang up so, I guess I'll call you back."

Beep-Beep...

"Yep, that's cool. Just know the ball's in your court."

Hanging up, Alexis rushed to her cell before her legs gave out from how excited she was. She even got down on her knees after the nightly count and prayed to God that what Stephon was kicking was real.

*****

In another unit of the detention center, Olivia was bidding. This was her second bid; her first drug case though. She didn't need nobody on the outside but her baby brother, Harold. He held all her cash, and had just put twenty grand on her inmate account. She knew she'd find herself a masculine dyke soon; one to suck on her pearl during the 84 months she'd pled out to earlier that day.

The prison time didn't faze her. To Olivia it was just a vacation. A small set back for a huge come back. That was what her first boyfriend told her when he caught 50 years in the feds. It was him who taught her to be strong.

She was laying on her back reading the latest novel by M.I. Waldo when her cellmate came in.

"Olivia, can you do me a favor?"

"What's up?" she asked, not looking away from her novel, that held her attention.

"I got an attorney visit, so I need you to hold down the poker table for me."

Sitting up, sliding her book marker in her book, she said "Okay."

Chapter 11

Danny had just finished doing 1000 push-ups. The 50 sets of 20 reps had his chest sitting up and out there. He was kind of fucked up about his aunt Olivia getting locked up, but Harold assured him that it was all just part of the game. What he was more lost on was his feelings toward Alexis. He was really feeling her. So when she wasn't answering his calls, and then started fucking with another dude, he let his love for her die. But now as he sat down on the back porch of his living quarters, catching his breath, rubbing Forbidden's paw, the love had come rushing back.

"What's wrong bae?" asked Monica, walking up, sitting on his lap. She rubbed her hands across the muscles around his neck and shoulders. They had become so close. Uncle Harold had let her move in with Danny well-knowing she would keep him grounded. Needless to say, she was halfway in love, and down for whatever.

"Nothing really...just thinking about the past. For real, like...I'm tryin' to understand why Lex calling me from jail when she left me in the wind. I'm not trying to answer that shit though."

Before responding, she placed his hand deep between her thighs, just so he would know how wet she was. "Oh, well maybe she realized how special you are."

Monica really didn't care for Alexis. It wasn't no beef or nothing. It's just the fact that the man she was feeling was still hurt over her. It made her not like Alexis. As they sat there in silence, Danny began fingering her with two fingers, just until his phone started ringing. Monica was on the verge of climaxing, and frowned when he stopped.

Seeing a '313' area code, Danny smiled.

"Hello, what's up?"

"Shit, I was calling to see if you still wanted to check them pups out," said the man on the other line.

"Recognizing the voice, Danny said, "Yeah, matter of fact, is it cool if I come up there?"

"Sure, shit and you can stick around to see the vicious work my bloodline put in. My bloodline shake the fleas off a bitch."

"Cool, I'll be up there tomorrow."

Ending the call, Danny wrapped his arms around Monica, kissed her neck, and told her they were going to Detroit.

"The Motor City? I never been."

"Yeah, well it's a first time for everything." Danny glanced over at Forbidden, "You gone be okay without us for a couple days, Forbidden?"

"Roof!" Forbidden barked, then he just continued licking his injured paw.

*****

Running around her bedroom, searching for her Coach shoes to match her handbag, Becky was too excited. Deeiaz had offered her to go on a trip with her and De'Audie. He informed her that this was to be somewhat of a pleasure trip, and to keep her mind open to any and all possibilities.

Hearing a horn blow outside, Becky peeked out her bedroom blinds to see a limo. A brown-skinned, bald brother was standing tall next to it.

"Well that's my ride, bye Lovely."

When they arrived at the airport they got on a sleek-shaped private plane that was loaded with gorgeous women of all nationalities. As Becky greeted the females, she recalled some of the females from the pictures Deeiaz had texted her. Getting to the front of the plane, she spotted Deeiaz and De'Audie chilling, sipping on Dom P., and smoking.

"Hey Becky, I'm glad you could make it."

"Me too, I'm excited. I see you got all your models here, so what's on the schedule?" she asked, taking a seat.

"Well, we have a photo shoot," Deeiaz explained. "But really we just out having fun."

"Oh, okay, well where we going?"

"To Detroit, you remember what I told you?"

"Yeah, I remember. Open mind, right." Becky smiled.

"Yes. Now here," Deeiaz passed her a yellow pill with a gun imprint on it. "Let's get this party started!"

"Becky took the pill, she threw it back without question. Then reclined her seat back, sipping on her drink, looking at the clouds they were flying above.

87

When they touched down, there was a convoy of limos awaiting. They were taken to a mini-mansion out in West Bloomfield, Michigan, an upscale suburban neighborhood.

As the girls all unpacked and begin readying themselves for their photo shoot, Deeiaz texted Becky: "Come down the hall."

At first Becky was helping everybody with the little things like make-up, but with that text, she was up and on the move.

"Deeiaz...you in here? It's me, Becky." Stepping in, closing the door, she heard a voice coming from the shower. Walking that way, she saw Deeiaz sitting on the edge of the tub giving De'Audie head. Stuck for a second, watching his large dick sliding in and out of Deeiaz's mouth, she bit her bottom lip with desire.

Enjoying the intensity of the oral sex Deeiaz was performing, De'Audie looked up with half-open eyes. Making eye contact with Becky he moaned, "You can come join."

Becky's nipples were hard; waiting for Deeiaz's approval, as she popped De'Audie's pole from her mouth, catching her breath. "You think you can hang?"

The effects of the ecstasy had kicked in an hour ago, Becky dropped to her knees and allowed De'Audie to sex her face. Gagging a few times as she tried to deep-throat him like Deeiaz was doing, when she felt a set of soft hands on her hips, ushering her ass up. Then came the joy of a tongue sliding across her clit.

"Ummm, sss! Ohh, yeah! Yeah!" Becky purred, before De'Audie pulled her head down, thrusting back into her mouth. With both hands, Becky began spreading her own cheeks apart, so Deeiaz could have complete access to her anus. At first she felt Deeiaz's tongue going up and down, then Becky felt a finger slide in. That did it! "Yess! Fuck, Deeiaz, I'm cumming," she cooed. Her juices of pleasure slowly dripping down her inner thighs.

Changing positions, De'Audie got behind Becky, and guided his swollen pipe inside her while Deeiaz sat on the sink.

"Suck my pussy good, Becky," Deeiaz ordered.

Becky was in heaven as the power couple took advantage of her. Bouncing her juicy ass back, in sync with De'Audie's stroke, she was fucking like she had something to prove.

"Oh, shit...Becky, damnit, I'm about to release my...oh dammit!" growled De'Audie as he repeatedly slammed his manhood totally into Becky's pulsating tight hole.

"Let me taste it," Becky cried, "please let me," she begged.

Just when he yanked out, she spun around catching some of his cum in her mouth, while the rest landed all over her chin and breasts.

Working her clit faster than the speed of light, Deeiaz skeeted all over Becky's ass. Her hips bucked up and down, as streams of warm sweet liquids released as if fired from a water gun. Becky turned back toward the waterfall, and bathed her face in it.

After that, Deeiaz and Becky tongue kissed, savoring the flavors of the moment, and De'Audie's warm semen.

*****

Chino had given everybody in the trenches the game plan: once the final couple keys were gone, they would start pressing the streets of St. Louis with the X-pills. Then branch out in neighboring cities. Chino would now be supplying his old Chicago connect, and hopefully every college kid in the Midwest.

Chino knew from popping the pills himself that all the dope boys would fuck with them. All that was left was to start hitting the universities and clubs with them, and tonight that was exactly what he was going to do.

Going over on the Eastside to a rave club called 'The Eyes', everybody inside was dancing, sweating, and seemingly hypnotized by glow lights the club owner was giving out. Females were kissing females, and Chino even saw two niggas kissing. Making his way through the crowd to the bar he saw a slim-thick amazon. She was about five-ten, and 135 pounds, with a skinny waist, and ass for weeks, with a beautiful caramel complexion and long hair.

"Hey! Let me get two double shots of Hennessy, and whatever she having."

As she bounced from foot to foot, Chino could see her tits jiggling.

"Thanks handsome," she said, "but what I'm off of ain't behind the counter." She sipped from a Smart water, looking so innocent.

"Oh yeah, and what you off, maybe we can help each other?" asked Chino, still sizing her ass up.

"E-pills."

With a grin he pulled out a 50 pack of the colorful tablets. Without a word, she pulled him off to a more secluded section of the club where another party seemed to be taking place.

"Me and my friend was just looking for some more skittles," she said while introducing him to everybody as "My candy man."

After filling 8 people's orders, the four 50 packs he'd come with were gone, just that fast. And the private party had just taken off!

Chino soon found himself sitting between two college chicks kissing, while they both played with his dick. With his hand beneath one of the girls' skirt he pulled her panties to the side and was about to beat her tight, barely-legal pussy to death, but when he heard a loud crash he jumped up and put his dick away.

"What was that?" he barked, his senses alert from the two double-stacked pills he'd swallowed.

He looked into the hallway noticing a big fight had broken out, but when he really focused in, he realized what was actually going on. "Oh shit, raid!" he yelled.

Scrambling now, he looked for a way out, when the two chicks grabbed his arm and said, "Follow us," in unison. When they popped out in the dark back alley, Chino was ready to go. I could have marked money on me, he thought, noticing a big rat shoot behind a nearby dumpster.

"Where you headed, sexy?" asked one of the girls. "Aren't you trying to finish what you started?" the other one questioned, poking her bottom lip out.

Looking at the both of them his dick got hard. "Yeah. But I need to do a drop off. Y'all driving?" he asked.

Shaking their heads 'no', Chino lead them to his whip. "I guess y'all rollin' with a real gangsta tonight then!"

*****

When Danny saw the midnight-black Razor pit bull with the white diamond on her chest, and the Gator pit with the head of a boulder, he knew this was it.

As he studied the two facing off in the box, he knew without a shadow of a doubt he was leaving with a pup from each kennel.

Instinctively the Gator preferred to be on the offensive attack, using it's power to pin down the Razor. The Gator's target was clearly the throat, and once it had the Razor by the underside of it's neck it began shaking it violently from side to side! "Let's go Gucci! Kill that bitch!" yelled the owner, crouched down on all fours.

The Razor wasn't too fazed by fighting from the bottom, it seemed to prefer it. Patiently it endured the punishment, and when the second the Gator thought ithad an easy victory, the Razor found a way to turn the tables around, as it spun, flipping the fatigued Gator on to it's stomach, as she worked the back of the other dog's neck. "That's daddy's bitch, work, work, work! Have fun momma, work!"

The Razor kept her fangs inches deep into the challenger's flesh, properly using a wide, hind leg base as a foundation. She shook and slung Gucci into the corner of the box inflicting serious punishment to Gucci's central nervous system. Then, in a fit of desperation Gucci sprang its front paws on to the rails of the box, trying to jump out!

"Rescratch!" yelled Gucci's owner.

Once both dogs were back in their corners, the ref yelled "Scratch!"

WIth no difference, Gucci body slammed the Razor, then maneuvered into the neck area and clamped down, shaking like she was trying to rip the dog's neck off. "Now squeeeezee! Come on. Squeeze!" Gucci's corner was sweating unceasingly, as the other beast used its leverage and broke the stranglehold, gripping a hold of Gucci's face! Unable to gain a breath of air, Gucci fell on the verge of suffocating, as she endured the painful torture!

Somehow Gucci was able to free her two eyes from the other dog's clutches in spite of all the free-flowing blood obstructing her vision. Lowering her striking point, Gucci struck her opponent's neck again, and unleashed a fury of unmerciful shakes that had the spectators screaming, and in a frenzy! A few minutes later, Gucci's contenders threw in the white towel, "Whoaaaaa, that's it!"

"Now that's what I call a real killa," said Danny before going over to the winner's kennel. Several men were busy tending to Gucci's near-fatal injuries. The owner emerged from the crowd of men, smiling, with sixty grand, all of which he won, and stuffed into a Gucci backpack that he slung around his shoulder.

"You like her style of fighting?"

"Yeah!" said Danny, "What's your name again?"

"Boog. So you still want to get a winning bloodline in your kennel?" He smirked.

"Hell yeah, Gucci a motherfucka in dat ring."

"Yeah, she represents 'Off The Chain Kennels' to the fullest. This is a winning brand. Are you in it to win?" He inched closer to face Danny, removing his friendly smile.

His time was money and if you wasn't about winning, and getting money, he had no conversation for you. He looked into Danny's eyes, searching...

"I'm in it to win, Boog. Straight up," assured Danny.

"I hope so. I don't got time for bullshit." Boog put an arm around Danny's shoulder and gave him an address. They talked a little longer before Danny decided to make a purchase.

"See you tonight," said Boog, shaking his hand.

Chapter 12

"So when we gone fuck around again?" Chino asked Becky while sitting in his stash house counting a table full of cash he'd dumped out. He was missing that good head she had on her shoulders. Plus he was trying to figure out why she'd been on some real distant shit lately.

"Shit, I don't know, I mean, I know you're busy with Melissa and Alexis. So when do you got time for me? Keep it real."

"You still on that shit! I told you I be serving Alexis work, and what's it matter, we just cool." He frowned.

"Right, we just cool, so all that freaky, kinky shit out the window, cause we just cool."

Chino hated when Becky got in her feelings, it wasn't like she didn't know he had other women in his life.

"Becky, ever since the day we pulled that sting you been on some real op shit. What's good?"

"Since you finally actin' like you're interested in me I'll tell you," Becky begin with. "For one, you treat me like anythang...like you don't care about me. You had me fuckin' dudes just so you could rob them. Then you treat Melissa like a queen, but I'm the bitch riding for you." Becky was on the edge of breaking down. He could hear it in her voice.

"I thought you was my gangsta bitch, Becky boo?" he said, hoping her pet name would ease her frustration.

It did a little. She paused. Smiled. Sniffled a little.

"I am, but you could respect me. Especially when I have your back all the time."

Chino knew it. She had a valid point. He'd been taking her for granted, but before he could even apologize or give her due credit, the line beeped in with Kilo on the other end.

"Becky, you right. Look though, I got a call to take. Where you at so I can scoop you, and take you out?"

"Whatever, Chino. I'm in Detroit. Just watch your back and be safe."

After he hung up, he wondered what she meant by "watch your back." Was she threatening his life on the low. He knew she had the heart to set a nigga up, but would she do him like that? he questioned himself.

"What's up my G?" answered Chino, still puzzled about Becky's comment.

"Hey folks, man we need to have a sit-down for real."

"Oh yeah, what's the topic?"

"On that one demo with you and Four."

Chapter 13

Alex was in the shower, when over the intercom came "Alexis Sims, visit. Sims, report to visitation."

"Here I come," she whispered to herself, drying off, rushing into her cell. She had been anxiously waiting for a whole month on this day. Before squeezing into her green uniform, she rubbed on some perfume- scented lotion she'd purchased from canteen. After that she nervously set her Bible on her locker, and headed to the unit officer's station.

Alexis scanned the visitation room once inside till her eyes landed on her prize. Stephon was donning a shape-fitting red, black and white Jordan jogging outfit, with retro 11s to match. Draping from his neck was a small diamond encrusted cross pendant, attached to a thin gold rope. His timepiece was a rose gold Rolex. Wasting no time, she jumped right into his arms.

"Hey sexy. I see you happy to see me." Stephon grinned, holding her tight, giving her a kiss.

"Umm, yes I am. I can't believe you really came," she cooed as they sat down across from each other.

"Come on ma. Don't do that, I told you I'ma be here for you."

With that, she smirked and they began kicking it about everything from what she did on a daily basis to how work was going for him.

"Bae, can I ask you somethin'?"

"Yeah, what's up?"

"What do you really do for a living?"

From the look he shot her, and by how he squirmed around in his chair, she knew he wasn't comfortable with her question. Alexis was from the streets and knew his life was more than just designing blueprints. She could feel the mysteriousness in his eyes.

"You sure that's what you want to talk about at a time and place like this?" he quizzed.

Reaching out for his hand, Alexis looked him directly in the eyes. "Stephon, my life is an open book. You know everything there is to know about me. And all I know is that you're my dreams come true. So, yes, I think it's the best time."

With a smile, he kissed her hand and said "Okay." By the time the visit was over, Alexis had a new perspective of him; his chain, and a promise that he would return tomorrow with a gift for her.

*****

As Becky walked up the river walk alone, she was enjoying its beautiful view of Detroit at night. Since she'd been kicking it with Deeiaz, she was becoming accustomed to a new way of life. After agreeing to becoming one of Deeiaz's models, things really got real. She gazed out at the star-filled skyline, reflecting.

"Becky before we go any further, I must let you know that it's more to our enterprise than just wearing panties and bras, and rocking the latest gear," expressed Deeiaz after another wild night of sex with her and De'Audie.

"I kind of knew that. So what's really going on?"

"Well, I've always told you to have an open mind. I've let you inside my sex life, my business, and now I offer you a chance to be involved in my MDMA distribution operation..."

Becky was utterly speechless initially, then she felt like there was no turning back. That's when she agreed to be all-in, for life.

Walking aimlessly past a stairwell, coming back to the moment she noticed a familiar face. Focusing in on it, she recalled who he was. "Danny, hey," she called out. "How's everything been?"

"Becky, damn, didn't think I would ever see you again. What you doing up here in the 'D'?" asked Danny, holding the leash connected to his new pit bull.

"Umm, well I'm here modeling. That's not the same doggie from that night is it?"

"Nawl," he said, smiling looking down at his beast. "I just got this one from these breeders up here. But what you got up doe?"

Thinking back to the night and circumstances when she met Danny, she thought about Chino, and Alexis fucking. Suddenly 'revenge' started screaming in her head. Becky had noticed Danny had bulked up considerably, and he had facial hair now. And his voice was so much deeper.

"Well I was actually planning on going clubbing tonight. You down?" she asked showing off her cleavage, and pearly whites.

"I'm going to check out a match later, but around 11-thirtyish would be cool."

"Good, it's a date then, take my number and call me later."

"Bet," he said, watching his dog sniffing at her feet.

*****

Chino looked at his fingertips as he was smoking a joint of Blue Cheese. He couldn't believe what Kilo had revealed to him. "*Man on Chief, folks, that bitch set that shit up.*" Kilo's every word kept replaying in his head like a broken record.

Kilo had hired a private investigator to look into the deceased dudes' backgrounds that tried to murder Chino. And as it turned out, those dudes were really somebody, and that was one of the reasons they hit his house like they did.

"*But bro, that ain't even the shit I really wanted to rap about*," said Kilo.

"Alright, well what's up? Speak yo' mind?"

"*Man you want to know how them niggas found out so fast that it was us?*"

Throwing a group photograph on the table, as Chino looked at it, he froze upon seeing a face that made him sick to his stomach. Standing between two of the men they had executed was Melissa.

"*These her people. I was fuckin' with this bitch that knew them guys, and she went to school with them. I'm telling you, these St. Louis hoes just as grimy as the niggas is, if not more.*"

Chino closed his eyes as the Blue Cheese expanded his thoughts. He was trying to figure out how to handle this situation.

He eased out two G-Spots (ecstasy pills) from his pocket and popped them into his mouth. Then he dialed up Kilo.

"What's up folks?" answered Kilo.

"Man, listen. I know how we gone play this shit. On chief, these country ass fuck-niggas gone see how it's done."

Chino hung up!

*****

Danny didn't really want to fight his new dog already. He hadn't even spent the whole day with his bitch. But Monica was more than eager to see what this Eli could do.

"Come on babe," she urged. "You never buy a game dog without game-testing it first. You didn't know that? It's not like it's a 'till the death' match." She laughed.

"We can't put her on the airplane cargo all chewed up, Monica."

"Hell, we'll keep the rental and drive it back if she gets ate up like that. Or hell, we'll just drive and leave her ass up here…"

Inside of a smoked out garage on the far Eastside with some thugs Boog knew, blunts were being passed around. All of the men shook hands, yet some signified their gang affiliation. One dude kept his eye on Monica. There was something about her he found very attractive.

Both dogs were young. Both about the same age, and not really conditioned for fighting yet. But game-testing was more about testing of a dog's heart and mentality.

The two dogs yapped and wiggled, as Danny noticed Boog strolling up with the swag of a confident black man. Meanwhile,

Monica was rifing through her purse and then made a $1,000 side bet with the man obsessed with her. He was sipping on a 40 ounce, and had a lazy left eye.

"You hold my grand sexy," he whispered, "and when your cur gets crushed, you gimme back two grand, plus you number. I'm trying to make you mines."

Before Monica could check his "your number" and "mines" comment, the ref yelled "Scratch!"

Danny's animal exploded out of his corner and powerfully fast, snatching the other dog's front leg, flipping her, then she began pulling and shaking! "That's it girl! Get that bitch!" coached Danny.

The other dog chewed on her aggressive attacker's head, as Danny's dog did a maneuver he'd only witnessed Gators do. Keeping her intensely tight grip, she rolled, causing the dog to lose her headlock, and then have to grapple defensively from the bottom.

"Let's go Ma-Ma!" screamed Danny. His animal's dominance was clearly evident as she worked.

Four brutal minutes into the match the ops asked for a "rescratch."

Danny got a firsthand look at why the opposing corner wasn't tripping when the beasts tangled up again, as if their animal was a bred wrestler. She used the strength of her paws, and legs, combined with her body weight to thrust Danny's bitch to her back, while mauling the side of her face!

"Now bite down Sheba, gotdamnit! Come on, show 'em what we 'bout!"

"Come on Ma-Ma, get up!"

ECSTASY

Hearing Danny's voice, his dog fought ferociously to get back up but was having a hard time.Sheba bit hard as a motherfucker! "Rescratch!Fuck that shit! Rescratch!"begged Danny, reaching out for a pair of breaking sticks.

Monica had her arms folded across her breast, observing the blood sport she loved so much. She was in diapers when she first witnessed a match, so her trained eye studied, analyzed, and perceived on a higher level.

Not wanting to continue the testing, Danny looked over at her.But her focus was on the animal in his arms who cried out for more action.She yearned for it." Aarrrrgh!!"

"Aye bro," Boog called out, "this what we gonna do. Face 'em away from each other. Then we gonna release them."

Confused, Danny asked "Why?"

"Because if she come out searchin' ready to hit, then she's a roller, Danny. And if she don't, then she's a fuckin' cur."

Monica nodded in agreement.

Doing as told, when they released the animals for the final time, Danny's dog shot around towards Sheba and they locked back up, ending with Sheba getting slammed. Sheba fought off the suffocating stranglehold with her legs as best she could. But asphyxiation began to set in and Sheba's limbs went weak and defenseless.

For the next 30 seconds Danny's fiend violently shook the fight out of her opponent!

"Yeah! Yeah, now that bad bitch a roller right there," one dude yelled out, pulling on a Newport. Exhaling smoke, with one eye squinted, he looked over at Danny, "Aye my nigga, what's the name of yo' kennel?"

Thinking of it, after observing his dog's ruthless style of warfare, and high off what he saw, Danny yelled "Ecstasy! Ecstasy Kennels!"

Danny and Boog shook hands and smiled at one another, while Monica stuck her tongue out at the man who lost the bet.

*****

While sitting in her VIP booth, Becky was thinking about the organization she was now a member of. She didn't want to be just a mule. She wanted to be a major player in this high stake game. So when Danny finally came bouncing through the club, and guys were dappin' him up, she figured he could help her ascend to the top.

"Becky what's up with you?"

"I'm great now that you're here. I thought you were going to stand me up."She smiled while getting up giving him a long warm embrace hoping he would see through her revealing outfit.

"Now why would I do that? That would be rude. Plus, you too damn pretty to stand up."

Seeing the sparkle of lust in his eyes as they conversed reminded Becky of the night they first met. After they romantically tapped their wine-filled glasses together in a toast, Becky asked. "Hey Danny, do you remember the night we met?"

With a wide grin, he said "How could I not."

Both laughing, she kept on with her spiel, "Well did you ever try those pills I left y'all?"

"Hell yeah, I did. Had me fuckin' the dog shit out of my chick." Danny laughed, but when he realized he was the only one laughing, he asked Becky, "What's wrong?"

The waitress came over with another bottle, setting it on the table. That gave Becky an opportunity to figure out how to control the situation without involving her emotions.

"What's up babygirl? What's on your mind?"

"It's been a long time since I was considered a 'baby'." She smiled sipping her drink. "But I'm trying to figure out why people like us are never fully appreciated."

"What you mean by that?" asked Danny.

"Well I remember how that night, you were willing to protect your girl, Alexis, at all cost. And I would do anything for Chino."

"And yo' point is?" Danny leaned back, folding his arms across his chest, and in doing so, his diamond chains rattled together.

Sensing Danny becoming irritated, she got down to the point of the matter.

"Well, I don't know if you know, or knew already, or even care, but Chino and Alexis, they're fucking. And I feel that loyal people like us shouldn't be mistreated like that."

Seeing Danny's nostrils flaring, his chest heaving, as he took in her words made her uncomfortable. She dug a hand down into her Chanel bag, finding her personal pill bottle filled with skittles. She popped two. Smiled. Then she thumped out two pills on a napkin in front of him. "Just forget I said that," she whispered, watching him chase the skittles down with his drink. "Danny, let's just have some fun here tonight." With that, Becky pulled him out to the dance floor.

The more the pills kicked in, the more they touched and felt on each other. She could feel the pressure of his hard dick against her booty as he grinded into her. The sensation was sending her hormones wild!

Danny gripped her small waist line, "So what was yo' point in telling me that?"

Reaching back with an arm, she gripped his head pulling his ear closer. She seductively whispered. "If you leave with me now," she kissed his ear, "I can tell you my purpose and more."

With curiosity aroused in his head, Danny exited with Becky.

Arriving at Becky's MGM suite overlooking the city, Danny flopped on the bed kicking off his Timbs. "Now talk," he asked her.

Loving the way he was taking control of the moment, Becky followed his order.

"Okay. First and foremost, I hate for somebody to use and abuse me. Honey, I'm not the type to get mad, I get even."

"So you tryin' to fuck?" he asked gripping his manhood with the cockiest of expressions.

"Yes. But I'm also trying to do business. And business comes before pleasure, right?" She began removing her leggings.

With a shocked look on his face, Danny asked, "What type of business?"

Becky didn't respond, she was putting her stilettos back on in spite of not having on anything else. As a tent formed in his pants,

Becky doggie-crawled up on his lap. His hands instantly wrapped around her ass cheeks.

"I see you know some people out here, and I need them connects for the business I'm in."

"You still ain't told me the business."

Leaning over, kissing him, circling her tongue across his neck and then into his earlobe had Danny's heart pounding like a jackhammer. Becky was looking so sexy tonight, Danny thought.

His hands continued with a slow exploration across the slopes and curves of her juicy ass. And her hips undulated back and forth like the waves of an ocean.

Their eyes locked at once. So when she moaned, "How do those pills have you feeling right now?" He knew then what the business was. "I've never felt this good in my life, right. Damn I'm winning. I'm free. Getting money. High. I mean what? You need me to push yo' pills? But shit, I'm not from up here. I'm here on dog business, Becky."

"But you move like you is. So what's that about?" She kissed his forehead, feeling his cock on her stomach begging to be sat on.

When Danny told her about the farm, him breeding fighting dogs, Becky knew she had to have him on her team. She saw his potential, and she just needed to set the stage. Then put him on it.

"That's great," she told him unbuckling his jeans. "The pills I'm going to give you, just give some away. The rest'll sell themselves. You'll be rolling in money, honey."

Doing away with the pants she knew he'd seriously think about her proposal. Yet, rather he agreed or not, she was about to get her some of his dick that was standing straight up. She took a single finger and circled her round areolas, and pink erect nipples as he gazed up into her blue eyes.

Taking his penis between her lips, his mind got cloudy. The fading thought of Monica at a nearby hotel, worried to death about his whereabouts drifted away.

"Shit that feels good," he groaned in awe, watching his entire dick vanish into Becky's mouth. After gliding his dick in and out, and back in, she eased it back out. Saliva rolled slowly down his shaft. And her chin. Then, she spit all over his dick, and pushed it back in her throat. They made eye contact. Then Becky bounced her face on it, deep throating him, and glided it gradually out.

"So what do you think?" she cooed, jacking him off, kissing the sides of his thick rod. Then as she awaited his reply, she squeezed it, and began smacking herself in the face with it. With her tongue, she lapped at the precum that began to seep from the head of his dick.

Grabbing the back of Becky's head forcing it back down, Danny said "We'll talk business later. Right now, it's time to get even."

Becky wouldn't have it no other way, in fact. Her moaning, and slurping sounds with such animal-like forcefulness and aggression was turning him on totally.

Pulling her up, he allowed her to sit her beautiful freshly-shaved split right on his face and lips. For the next 30-minutes, Danny ate his way up to her big heart, and beyond.

"Wooo! Ummm Danny. Yes, suck that pussy boy. Fuck yeah!" Shuddering like she'd been electrocuted, Becky began to reach an orgasm. "Ahhh! Ahh! Danny!"

Danny then maneuvered his thumb into her tight virgin-like anus, causing both, an anal and clitoral orgasm at the same time. Becky rode his face like a mad bull, a tear of ecstasy trickling down her soft ivory face.

After resting her trembling body across the bed, Danny took a good swig of the bottled water on the nightstand. "I hope you ready. Because tonight I'ma bring the true slut out of you." Before penetrating Becky, Danny took the head of his pleasure stick and circled the entrance of her vagina. "Did you hear what I said?" he asked with a cunning smile.

"Bring it on daddy." She added, "I'm your slut tonight."

Chapter 14

What Chino couldn't understand was, where was Melissa at. And who the hell was this dead chick with her eyes and mouth wide open in the bathtub.

Kilo looked down at her, "Oh shit, that's shorty that told me about Melissa." He covered his mouth, lost in thought at the discovery.

"How the fuck you know, folks?" he asked, now gazing at the big hole in her forehead.

"Because of that right there," Kilo replied, pointing at the rosary beads tattooed across her breasts.

Going into the bedroom that he and Melissa shared, Chino noticed all her things were gone. I mean the girl didn't even forget a pair of dirty socks. She had bleached all of his shoes and hats, and left behind a "Dear John" letter sitting neatly folded on the dresser. Chino picked it up, unfolded it.

It read: "I guess the cat's out of the bag. I never liked that bitch anyway. I had told my brother that bitch was not to be trusted. Honestly, I wish your ass would have listened when I told you to fall back, but you didn't. So now that my cousin and brother is dead, it's war and your turn is next! So if your stupid ass still at the house, which I figure you is, this is good bye. It was fun while it lasted."

Balling up the note, about to toss it, but before he could, the fireworks started!

Boom! Boooom!!! Bloc! Bloc!! Bloc!!! Blocca!!!

Hearing the automatic-style gunfire was nothing compared to feeling the vibrations, and seeing the destruction sent through the house! Walls ripped apart, the TV set exploded, windows came shattering down as Chino dove for cover beneath the bed, praying it wouldn't be his death-bed. Suddenly the shooting ceased. Crawling to his feet, Chino darted down the hallway with his Glock in hand, overcome with paranoia and fear!

"Kilo! Aye folks! Kilo? Where you at joe?"

Making his way across glass shards scattered all over the living room floor, his heart dropped down in his ass, as Chino crumpled to his knees. "Nooo!! Come on folks, don't do this. C'mon gangsta. Don't leave me like this!" He threw up his forks to Kilo, but Kilo was unable to throw them back this time. And for the first time, since the age of nine, Chino cried a river, as his hands trembled like an autumn leaf blowing in the wind. He knew the cops would soon arrive, asking questions. He had to go!

Kilo had taken six shots to the chest, and one to the right eye, knocking the back of his head off. They had grown up together, brothers, gangstas. And now, he was gone. Sirens could be heard blaring in the distance.

"It's okay G, I swear, on Larry, I'ma kill dat bitch! I swear!"

Just then, as he was saying his final farewells, the dining room window came crashing in! Clutching his pistol, waiting for a nigga to jump is when he noticed orange lights flickering off the walls. He set Kilo's shell of a body down, scurrying to check it out. Smoke filled his lungs!

"Oh shit! Fuck!" he exclaimed.

Seeing flames engulfing everything they touched drove Chino back into the living room where he then tried desperately to pull Kilo with him, when there was a silence.

Boooom! Boom! Boom!!

Hitting the floor when more shots rang out, sending blinding shreds of drywall and wood chips everywhere, he realized his only two options. Either leave Kilo G, or die with him tonight. Flames of death were consuming the house. Chino could hear the killers slamming a car's doors, followed by another distant round of gunfire. "I swear, on Larry, my nigga!" were Chino's last words as he burst out the back door, licking shots in the darkness. But they were already gone. He never even looked back as he ran deep into the St. Louis night, coughing. And crying.

*****

3 years later…

After getting a 68 months sentence, Alexis was ready to get this over with. Even with Stephon being there for her, and bringing her weed every visit wasn't enough to soothe the agony of being confined. She could never get used to the degrading feeling of getting cuffed up everywhere she went.

As the days drifted by, all she could think about was how Stephon was her knight in shining armor. He never missed a visit, he sent pictures, money, and even wrote her love letters.

Doing her time at a sweet federal prison camp in Greenville, Illinois made it all possible for Alexis and Stephon to get tight. The Federal Bureau of Prisons sent Olivia way out to Aliceville, Alabama to do her 120 months, but they kept in contact through email. Seeing they were co-defendants Alexis' case manager made it possible. Olivia's words were inspiring, because she carried the burden of doing time like it wasn't nothing. Olivia had made mention that Harold and Danny kept her straight, so she was good, and she even had her a new girlfriend too.

At the mentioning of Danny, Alexis began wondering why he never accepted her calls or wrote her. Initially she felt it was because he was on the run for killing Sugar Man, and them. But when Olivia said she be talking to him all the time, she snapped. "That's crazy, he act like I did something to him," she vented to her cellie, Crystal.

"I mean you know how niggas is, one minute they loyal, the next, they nose up some other bitch skirt." Crystal and Alexis both laughed at what the deemed the truth.

"But still," said Alexis.

"Plus didn't you say y'all wasn't fuckin' around after he left town?"

Alexis had never told her cellie the real reason why Danny left the city for fear that Crystal would snitch to authorities in order to get a sentence reduction.

"Yeah I get it," she expressed, "but still he could at least accept my calls, like, we ain't beefing."

That was the only thing that slowed her time down, because she felt he owed her an explanation.

Stephon had even paid Alexis's mom's air fare to and from for visits between them, as well as her, now, teenage daughter. She was hoping that upon her release from prison, her mother and daughter would be willing to move down to St. Louis. But that was only a dream, a wish. New York had more to offer, Alexis thought.

That day had finally arrived for Alexis to report to 'R&D'. (Receiving and Discharge) Earlier that morning she wrote Danny's name on her list of people to see.

"Well Ms. Sims today's the day. How you feel?" asked her case manager.

"I feel great! I'm finally about to get back to my life. Back to money-making and having fun."She gave a big Kool-Aid smile.

Nervous, fidgeting around with her engagement ring she was recalling the day Stephon had proposed. "Well I got to keep it one-thousand with you Lex. I'm truly in love with you. These 3-years have been the best of my life. And I'll be a fool to not lock you down." With that, Stephon knelt to one knee and pulled out a gorgeous ring that lit up the visitation room, taking her breath away. "Alexis, I never thought I would find my soulmate and now that I have. Will you marry me?"

"Mrs. Sims, Mrs. Sims!" yelled her case manager, pulling her out of the pleasure of remembrance. "I'm sorry. I was… gone." She smiled, stepping out of the institution's front door.

Besides the sunshine, the first thing Alexis saw was her husband-to-be leaning up against a candy apple red Lexus, smiling.

"So they finally let my queen out." Running towards him, she leaped up wrapping herself around him.

"Yes baby," she began with, "and I'm here to stay."

"Good cause bands got to be collected." After stopping to see her supervised release officer, they rode around the city for a while, finally pulling into Ruth Chris; one of the best steakhouses in St. Louis. While awaiting their meals, they smiled, flirted laughed and were enjoying one another's company, until he got a call on his cell phone.

"Yeah. Alright. Give me like an hour, and I'll be on my way... because my wife just came home! Yup." He sat his phone down after glancing at the time.

"So let me guess, where do I want you to drop me off at, huh?" asked Alexis, somewhat pissed off.

"Why would I drop you off, that's your car."

"You for real Stephon?"

"Yes, and I'm sorry I have to go but I promise, tonight will be all about you."

Smiling at Stephon as he handed her the key pad to the Lexus, she said "I love you."

"I love you too." He smiled. "Now come on, It's time you drop me off, I have important business to tend to."

Chapter 15

After the night with Becky, Danny decided to stay in the city. He turned Detroit into his second home. Monica didn't object, so they found some open space of land out in Ypsilanti, Michigan, where that became his compound for Ecstasy Kennels. The property sat secluded near a women's prison, and getting into the heart of Detroit wasn't but a twenty-minute ride.

Danny never told Becky in detail about the bodies, and the child he left dead in the projects. But being in Detroit now, he rarely thought about it. Thinking about how he was going to secure his next five-hundred grand was the only thing on his mind on this summer night.

As he strolled through 'The Hole In The Wall' nightclub, Danny used a finger to push up his Cartier frames more on his nose. He caught a glimpse of the two chicks on the dance floor damn near getting it in. After sitting at the bar, he asked a sexy young bartender for a bottle of Hennessy, and dropped three-hundred-dollar bills.

"Keep the change, sweetheart."

That's when a man's voice said, "I see you really feeling yo'self."

Danny smiled seeing it was Frankie, the club owner. They had gotten cool a year ago when Frankie first opened.

It didn't take rocket science to notice that every time Danny showed up, the club sold out of bottled water and bar sales would triple. One night, months prior, Frankie had pulled down on Danny, introducing himself. He gave Danny the title of "Royalty" in the club.

"What's up bro?" said Danny with a little swag in his voice.

"Shit, my bank account and sales."

"Okay playa, so what brings the big man so close to the dance floor?" Danny grabbed his bottle.

"For one, to tell you to leave my bartender alone. She's mine. And I need to discuss some business wit'cha."

After a grin, Danny took a gulp from his bottle, pushed his glasses up and told Frankie to "Lead the way." When they entered Frankie's sound proof office, Danny walked over to the huge saltwater fish tank and studied the baby sharks swimming in circles, waiting for their next prey.

"Tell me something good," asked Danny turning to face Frankie, taking another gulp of the Henny.

"Alright so currently I'm getting seven jars from you. But I'm tryin' to double that."

"Okay. What's the problem?"

"Well, I'll tell you," he began with "you charging me three dollars a pill."

"And?"

"I'm trying to get that down to two."

With a somber look, Danny sat his bottle down and pulled out his phone. Doing the math, he felt comfortable with the resulting number. But he knew it could be better, so he sat on Frankie's leather chair and said "How about $2.50, and I front you six jars?"

Thinking it over, Frankie fired up a blunt that filled the office with the scent of exotic cush. Passing the blunt as he did his math in his head, he said, "That sounds like a playa's deal." Frankie just sat there as he began exhaling smoke from his nostrils.

Leaving out of Frankie's office, Danny was good and tipsy, but not too intoxicated to get caught slippin'. While making his way back to the bar he peeped two large black guys stalking him. They whispered to one another then both their eyes zeroed in on Danny in sync. Playing his role, pretending to be pissy drunk, he detoured stumbling to the restroom. He texted Monica, who was in VIP with: "Boo go start the car it's time to go, and watch yo'self!"

The very second, he hit 'send' the bathroom door came flying open. Looking over his shoulder as he pocketed his cellphone, he noticed the same two dudes.

"What up doe? Aye, you got some E's my guy?" asked one of them.

"Nawl I'm all out dude."

As Danny turned around, he saw one of the men reaching, so he did the same. Pulling out his Glock 43, he started firing from the hip. The high caliber Glock sounded like thunder! Boom! Boom! Bang! Bang!

Club patrons screamed and scrambled outside the bathroom door, as Danny leaned against a urinal, feeling a sharp pain in his thigh. One of the men clutched his stomach, and slid down the wall into a fetal position. His partner jetted out the door. "Fuck!" yelled Danny, noticing the small hole in his Louis Vuitton jumpsuit.

Looking down at the nigga he'd hit on the floor of the bathroom, squirming and begging for help, Danny aimed his pistol at him.

"Please man, please. I got kids to feed."

"Yeah, and I got a reputation to protect."

Boom! Boom!

"Pussy!" spat Danny, stuffing his pistol in his pants, limping out to the parking lot where Monica was waiting in his black Charger. Danny dove in, not even closing the door behind him when he screamed "Pull off!"

Stopping at the first red light before finally shooting through it, Monica asked "What happened?"

"Some black ass niggas tried to rob me!" he cried, gritting his teeth.

"Danny, oh my god. You're bleeding! They shot you."

"No shit!" he grunted. "This shit burn like a motherfucker."

"We got to get you to the hospital," she said, making a right in the direction of St. John's Hospital.

"Hell nawl, I deaded one of those bitch boys."

"Well if we don't you might bleed to death, what if an artery's been hit?"

Too preoccupied by the agonizing pain to speak, Danny blazed up a Black'N'Mild. He took a hard pull on it. Exhaled the smoke. "Shit! Let's go to the compound. I've seen you sew up plenty of wounds after dog fights. We got everything we need there. I just hope the bullet went in and out. Don't let me die tonight boo."

They rode in silence. Monica felt that ever since Danny had gotten in the pill game it was always something. Either him evading the cops, to some nights he didn't come home at all. And now he'd been shot. She gazed over at him, and she could tell, he was addicted to this lifestyle, and didn't plan to give it up.

Chapter 16

Life for Chino had finally started to get better. He was still hunting for Melissa. Word on the streets was, she fled to Atlanta. He was still at war with the Crips, having recently slumped a few in a motorcycle drive-by in broad daylight.

With Audie supplying him with the skittles and him getting back to the bricks of coke, his check was all the way up.

Pulling up to one of his traps to collect, and drop off, Chino saw a ghost from his past. Crossing the street to get a better view of her he asked, "Alexis, is that you?"

"Chino! Oh my god it's been forever. How you been?" She hugged him, as she was just leaving the hair salon.

"I'm good. You know me, hustle and finesse. Where you been? You glowin' and shit."

"Well if you must know, I'd gotten locked up. I just got out the feds a few months ago."

Hearing that was a shocker, the whole time he thought she went back to New York. He began sizing her up, licking his lips, remembering what she tasted like.

"Oh yeah well it's good to see you again. Welcome home."

"Yeah, same here," she giggled. "Thank you."

Reaching into his jeans pocket, Chino eased out a big knot of bills. He peeled her off a grand, "Here. This is how you welcome home a beautiful woman. Now can I take you out for a drink or something so we can catch up?"

Holding the cash, smiling, flashing her diamond engagement ring, Chino knew what it meant. But that didn't change his mind about what he wanted.

"Okay. How about a friendly drink. Is that cool? And thank you for the donation."

"That's fine," he said, looking at the growing cluster of guys standing outside his trap house. "I need to handle something real quick. Were you–"

Alexis cut in with, "Go ahead, I'll be sitting right here in my car waiting for you."

Chino ran across the street, as all his soldiers followed him inside. He returned a short while later and motioned for her to follow his black Range Rover. But she climbed out and chirped her auto alarm and eased up into the truck, behind his dark tint. That's when Chino peeled off into traffic. They began chopping it up about what's been going on in each other's lives and getting lost in nostalgia, and laughter.

Working on their second round of drinks, both their cellphones rang at the same time. One of Chino's lookouts had texted him that he'd seen some Crips piled up in a white cargo van on Bosten Rd. Since that wasn't but up the street, Chino stood up ready to dip.

"Umm, Chino. That was my fiancé. He wants to spend some quality time," she said in a defeated tone.

"It's cool, I got a move to shoot anyway. Let's go. Maybe we can catch up later!"

Doing 80 miles per hour on a side street, Alexis couldn't wait to get the hell out the truck.

"I see you really in a rush," she made mention, as he shot through a red light.

"Yeah, it's something really important."

Every chance Chino got an opportunity to kidnap a Crip he would torture them, trying to get a lead on Melissa. Even with placing 50-grand on her head, nobody was talking.

He broke his speed down, pulling up just beside her Lexus, eyeballing his rearview mirror.

"What's your number?"

"I told you, I'm engaged." She smirked.

"Oh yeah, I told you I just want to be a friend."

She looked at him like 'yeah, whatever,' and said "What's your number? I'll call you. How about that?"

Giving her his digits, he was back in traffic, on the phone with his hitta named LA. He made his way over LA's neighborhood and dialed him up.

"What's up big homie?" asked LA.

"Aye I'm coming down the block in 5 minutes, come out with that bitch!"

"Bet."

Hitting a couple corners, Chino pulled to a stop at a corner house where a lanky brown-skinned dude with salt and pepper waves ran out with a T-shirt wrapped around an M-16. LA was puffing on a blunt, "What's up my G?" he asked climbing up inside the truck.

"The guys said they saw some crabs on Bosten in a white van." With that being said, the vibe in the truck switched to a deadly one, indeed.

A text came in to Chino's phone. It was from one of the guys. "Aye, they out here flagging!"

"Where?"

Just then, LA patted Chino's thigh, "Look!" There was a Buick parked, and a guy with a blue bandana around his neck climbed out, followed by a guy with one around his left wrist. Then, as the white van crept up beside the two men, LA pulled a ski mask over his face. Chino reached beneath the driver's seat for his Drayco, sending a round into the chamber. Then he disengaged the safety with this thumb. They both slithered out of the truck with stealth.

"Oh shit cuz!" was all the Crip got out his mouth before Chino and LA released hell upon them! Sparing no Crip, as twisted bodies fell, and were sprawled across the streets in a gruesome display of tribal vengeance.Making their exit the same way they came, Chino bobbed his head in sync to the music. In his mind, this was only one day, on a list of many to go. "On Larry, Kilo!" he mumbled to himself, dropping LA off and heading to his low-key spot in Fergeson.

*****

"License, registration, and proof of insurance ma'am," asked the police officer. He stood there peering down into the cabin of Becky's silver G-Wagon.

Becky was a little paranoid; she had a baggie full of ecstasy pills in her glove box. Slowly she reached over fidgeting with the glove box, making sure her skirt was hiked completely up revealing all of her ass. That did it, she slammed the glove box back and handed the cop what he'd asked for.

"Did I do something wrong?" she asked, biting her finger.

"You made an illegal turn back there, then you were doing 55 on a 35 mile per hour street."

Becky knew she was moving a little too fast, yet the money was coming in so fast. And she was in the fast lane of life. She had a guy waiting on 1-thousand pills. "Oh, I'm so sorry," she lied. "I'm trying to get to my mother, she fell down the stairs and now she's in the hospital."

That was pretty much all it took for Becky to wrap the traffic cop around her finger. They exchanged numbers, and after saying "Thank you handsome," she brought her Benz to life and began carefully merging into traffic. When her phone rang, she knew it was Kenny, her buyer. "I'm right around the corner. Yeah, I got that... alright, come outside. Yeah, that's me."

Pulling up to the curb, Kenny jumped in, and she pulled off. "Damn baby gurl, I thought we was finna handle business?" he questioned.

"We are, now count out that cash."

As Becky circled a few blocks as a safety precaution, while Kenny counted the cash, she pulled over not far from her old college apartment. Seeing the money was all there, she put it all inside her truck's center console and pointed him to the glove compartment. Seeing all the skittles, Kenny slid the baggie in his pocket. As Becky dropped him off and Kenny was stepping out the truck, someone called out her name.

"Hey Chino, what you doing over this way?" She rolled her window down.

"Damn it's been a minute since I've seen you," he said walking up to her window. "But boo, you know this my block. What's up my G?" he stated greeting Kenny.

"Living life, aye Becky, I'll holler."

Chino seemed to take sudden interest in Kenny and followed him, "Chino it was good seeing you." Driving off, Becky texted Danny, letting him know they needed to talk. Even though they were on a business level, she loved the way he put the dick down.

Laughing at Danny's reply to her text at a red light, is when she looked over seeing Chino's truck beside her. "You following me or something?" she yelled over at him.

"Bitch! Ain't nobody following you. You the one popped up on my strip. What you selling? … on my blocks?"

"And if I am, then what?" she challenged.

"Don't play. You know what it is. So stop playin' tough before I whack your little boyfriend."

"He's not my boyfriend, he's a client, now what?"

Hearing horns blowing, combined with the look of fury in Chino's eyes gave Becky cause to peel off!

Chapter 17

Danny was damn near back walking straight again. He knew he was a person of interest after the Detroit Homicide Unit began investigating the body found in the club bathroom. But there could be no talking with the police, not with his past, and present criminal activities. After getting a call from Becky he was ready to hit the road and spend some time in the country. He'd still be a hop and a skip away from St. Louis. Plus this would give him an opportunity to spend time at Uncle Harold's too.

After making sure all his hounds were straight, and giving orders to the dog workers, Danny took off his muddy boots. And while limping inside, he yelled, "Aye Monnie, pack me like 50-grand so I can get me some clothes."

"Baby, I thought you wasn't coming."

"I changed my mind," he began with, "I can't miss a chance to see the kennel. I miss the babies down there."

"Well," she embraced Danny. "Since you're coming, I might as well tell you."

"Tell me what?" asked Danny.

"I'm in the process of lining up a match," she revealed while playing with one of her rings.

"Yeah, with who?"

"Tina Marie. Me and pops got into it and one thing lead to another."

Danny paused thinking about the situation. Tina Marie was a four time killer like himself, he thought. But he wasn't mad, she was old, but well experienced.

"I'm all for it. White dogs got no place in the ring. Tina Marie, she's a freak of nature. Monica, what's the wager, because yo' pops not gone roll that bitch for anything under seventy-five thousand."

Monica began stuffing a few more items in her bags, pretending not to hear Danny's question.

"How much?"

"Okay! One-hundred-grand."

Smiling, Danny knew Ma-Ma was more than Tina Marie's equal. From the scratch with Sheba, Ma-Ma turned into a certified chest and neck dog.

As they rode down the Interstate, Danny reclined his seat back and began reading the latest Sporting Dog Journal. Meanwhile, Monica was eating up the highway, looking cute in some large Chanel shades. Leaving Detroit behind and all the drama that came with it now had Danny asleep over in the passenger seat.

"Pump the gas sleepy head!" barked Monica.

Danny woke up realizing they'd made it there. While pumping gas he didn't pay much attention to the slim thick young lady pumping gas across from him. His mind was on getting Ma-Ma in fighting shape, which would take at least 8 weeks.

"Hey stranger," said Alexis, standing in front of him.

"Them was my same thoughts. How life been treatin' ya?"

"Good. So what happen to you?" she asked with her hands on her hips.

"What you mean?"

"I mean you couldn't write me, or accept my calls. Like what type of hoe shit was you on?"

Gritting his teeth and keeping his emotions in check, he began to feel buried feelings and then the sting of her abandoning him. "The same hoe shit you was on when I buried them fuck niggas behind you. Then you started fuckin' some other nigga, and not answering my calls."

Alexis could tell Danny wasn't the same anymore. From his weight gain, tattoos, and a new swag. To her, she could feel the heat of the flames burning in his eyes.

"Listen Danny. I didn't know.Look, get in my car, let's go somewhere and talk."

Even though everything about the situation screamed 'No!' in his head, his past feelings wouldn't allow it.

"Lex, I'm only going to be here for a few days. So I guess before I leave we can sit down and end this chapter of our lives."

Her face twisted when she said, "How do you figure this the end?"

"Because that ring on your finger don't scream 'promise ring.'"

Laughing at the obvious, she gave him her number and they parted ways.

Climbing into the car Danny asked Monica "When and where will the match take place?"

"Who the hell was that bitch Danny! See that's what I'm talkin' about. You don't fuckin' respect me!"

"Man, stop trippin'. That was Alexis."

"And! So what, cause that's yo' ex-bitch it makes it fuckin' alright to talk to her? You got me fucked up."

Shaking his head Danny shot a text to Uncle Harold's phone, letting him know he'd be in his quarters on the compound for a few days. Harold returned his text with a smiley face.

The rest of the ride Monica kept venting, even speaking in Spanish at times. Danny kept quiet, thinking of the match, and the hard biting white bitch Tina Marie. After rolling a blunt of Blue Cheese he chilled.

When they arrived, happily barking muscle-bound dogs welcomed them. Danny made his way to the rear of his domain, thrilled with the Jeep, and Redboy Jocko bloodline. But Ma-Ma's viciousness made Danny welcome the Eli line with open arms.

Uncle Harold showed up later in a pair of coveralls, looking like a black Incredible Hulk. After giving Danny a man-hug, and kissing Monica's hand, they joked around about the business of game dogs. Both daring the other to put up or shut up. When Harold was about to leave Danny asked to ride with him. That's when Monica stood up and asked, with a slight attitude, "Is you goin' to be back before the day is up?"

"Yes Baby. And we gone kick it okay."

Hearing the sincere love in his voice she smiled and said "Okay."

Jumping in Harold's truck Danny realized this was the same Cadillac from back in the day. "Damn Unc. What's it getting hard out here?"

"Why you ask that?"

"Because I'm sayin' you done had this bitch forever!"

"I see yo' half-breed asss done went up to Detroit and got a sense of humor."

They both laughed. Danny started rolling up a blunt and caught Uncle Harold looking out the corner of his eye a few times as they rode on. After firing up the blunt Danny began to consider the situation, he had to contend with that Becky had brewing. Catching Uncle Harold peeking over at him again, Danny said "What's up Unc? What's on yo' mind?"

"Nawl, I just see you shining with the Rollie, big boy designer wear, and the icy Carties."

Smiling at the acknowledgement, Danny said "Shidd, I'm just enjoying the fruits of my labor."

"Yeah, I see. Shitt, let a country nigga like me hold something till I see better days, nephew."

"I got you Unc. Let me just holla at my people first and I'ma get with you."

Calling up Becky, he told her to come scoop him so they could discuss the Chino situation.

As Danny hung up he thought about how lately, Becky had been using pet nicknames. Like the last time they met, she was actually pressing him out for sex, and after, she wanted to cuddle up.

Seeing Becky's silver G-Wagon pulling up brought Danny's mind to the present moment. He peeled Harold off about 3-grand and jumped in her truck.

She pulled off headed towards St. Louis.

"What's up shorty? You alright?" asked Danny, smelling the sweet scent of perfume and prosperity. He began craving to hold onto her.

"Hey boo, I'm okay." She smiled. "I just don't like how Chino pulled that stunt. And he had the audacity to make my customers move off the block."

"Yeah? Damn, dude wild'n huh? So where do I come into play with all of this?" asked Danny, reclining his seat back.

"Well Danny, I'm your supplier. If I got a problem, then at some point, you got a problem."

"How you figure?" he began with. "I don't got shit to do with that. You didn't get shot with me!"

Becky got quiet, then hit him with "So how you figure you're going to get anything if I have a situation, and can't supply you. In turn, you can't supply the streets. There's levels to this shit boo."

"You got a point." He turned his head away. "So Becky, how do you suggest we handle this?" asked Danny, as they pulled up into the driveway of her home.

Saying nothing, Becky stormed out the car and into the house.

Once inside, Danny found her at her bar sipping from a bottle of Grey Goose. She looked mad at the world.

"Becky, what the hell is wrong with you, huh?"

"My problem is, men always try to walk over me or use me!"

With that, Danny shook his head, he knew the dope game was a man's game, yet, he also knew this was more than Chino.

"Okay, now I'm lost. Did you call me here to find a way to deal with Chino? Or is this about something else?"

"Danny, I've helped you take your hustle and life to a higher level," she reminded him, coming from around the bar. She stood right there in front of him. "I've let you have your way with me, and I respect you as a business partner and as a man."

"Okay Becky! And you act like you not getting nothing out of this. So what's up?"

"What's up you ask. What's up, is I'm trying to understand why you haven't made me your woman yet?"

With a blank face Danny just stared at her frustrated beauty. He knew this was going to come up sooner than later, and it had.

"Listen Becky, what we got is good, and everything, and I'm thankful for the chance you gave me. But I'm with somebody."

"Yeah, but you didn't care when I was allowing you to fuck me in every hole on my body!"

"You right. I didn't. I'm wrong for that. But shorty been here for me the long way, for a long time. You feel me?"

With a frown, slumped shoulders, and now hands on her hips, she lifted her chin up and asked "Where does that leave me?"

Not trying to hurt her feelings, and lose his dream plug all at once, Danny carefully made his words comforting to her emotions.

"I don't know," he pulled her close. "I'm feeling everything about you. But I can't bring myself to do shorty how Alexis did me." He kissed her, strumming his hand through her lustrous hair. "I just don't know. Let me sleep on it okay."

Twisting her lips up in a way that said she didn't really believe him, she replied with "Okay Danny. Okay. But you better think on it. And I thank you for being understanding. I'm the kind of woman that requires security, that's all. Think on it."

"I will. Now let's solve this Chino problem my baby having."

Chapter 18

"Arrre, yess!! Fuck, baby... shit!" moaned Alexis, as Stephon drilled away, while she laid on her side. Pulling his glazed dick out of her, he ordered her to, "Suck them love juices off." Crawling closer to him, she did just that.

When Stephon started playing with her pussy, she was drooling at the mouth, taking him completely in, doing her best deep throat performance.

"Fuck bae!" He felt his rod about to release, dripping sweat, Stephon pushed a purple ecstasy pill and his middle finger deep inside her ass.

She was loving how he was fingering her asshole, making her pussy ooze with sweet cream. After kissing the entrance of her anus, Stephon replaced his finger with his tongue. Gripping and spreading her cheeks apart, feeling her pussy contracting, as he tongue-fucked her asshole, he knew she was ready to get pounded with his 9-inches.

For the next 45-minutes Stephon made constant contact with Alexis' G-Spot, leaving the sheets soaked. Alexis screamed, clutching the wet sheets as he nailed her, "Shittt! ah, ah, ah, god, fuck, damn!" she screamed out, trembling like she was being struck by lightning. Finally, Stephon flipped her up on all fours, getting the perfect view. He wrapped her hair around both his hands, pulling her head up, beating her pussy until he shot off his load inside her.

They cuddled; panting, drained and thirsty. After wrapping her leg around his, Alexis asked, "Bae, when you gettin' out the game?"

"When I hit a lick that can keep me from robbing," he said rolling out the bed. He walked into the bathroom.

Alexis always stressed how she wasn't cool with him robbing. Selling drugs, 'yeah', but robbing, 'no'. Not after what happened with Danny.

"So you sayin' if I can put you on a good lick then you won't go robbing with yo' uncle no more?"

He stepped back in the room, his dick still semi-hard, catching Alexis' attention. "Alexis, what you saying…you got a lick, and you ain't told me?"

Stephon crawled back in bed, between her thighs, kissing on her pearl. Losing herself in the moment, Alexis cooed, "Nooo, yess." She zoned totally out until she began creaming again all over his face.

It was like Stephon knew how to get her climax to its peak. Like he was the master of her body. While on her back, spreading her legs apart, as if she was doing the splits, he fed her vagina every inch, and some in a push-up position. After beating her walls this way, they both screamed out every cuss word imaginable.

"I'm 'bout to cum. Oh shit!" growled Stephon, filling her center with his warm semen.

Rolling up a blunt after they'd showered, Stephon brought up the topic about her having a lick.

"Well I think I do, but first I got to do my homework on it."

She accepted the blunt, hit it once, passing it back, knowing she had an upcoming piss test. After coughing, she said "Well this dude I used to talk to before going to prison been shooting at me the last month. And I noticed he still in the game, moving something…what?" She paused, seeing the frown on his face.

"So you been kickin' it with your ex?"

"No! Baby, he not exactly my ex, yeah we messed around but I was fuckin' him for a lower price on the coke I was buyin' from him."

"Yeah Lex, whatever," he replied, exhaling smoke from his nostrils like a dragon.

"Come on baby," she got closer. "You don't have nothing to worry about. You are the only man for me." She eased herself onto his lap.

"Well if it ain't really about shit, then why I'm just finding out?"

"Okay you're right. I'm sorry. But just know it's really nothing. I'm all yours."

She kissed Stephon.

When they both heard Lil Boosie's song: 'Say Round' playing, they both knew who it was, and what time it was. Stephon reached over toward his cell phone, "Ma, you know I got to answer that."

"Yeah, I guess, whatever," replied Alexis as she stormed into the kitchen for something to eat.

Once Stephon was dressed he gave Alexis a hug from behind, kissed her neck, said, "I love you," and walked out.

After squeezing into a pair of boyshorts, on the leather sofa, scrolling through Facebook on her cell phone, Alexis smiled. She continued to look through her daughter's photos on her page. Next she decided to see if Danny still had his page up. Seeing that it wasn't she slumped down. "Figures. Why didn't I get his number," she asked herself.

Alexis didn't know why, but seeing Danny all grown up, buff and mature-looking was on her mind. All her anger seemingly turned to lust. It had been years since they had even talked to one another. She'd come to realize the reason she started avoiding him in the first place was because she was shocked he could kill a child with no remorse. As she sat there thinking back to that dark night, he called.

"Hello, who is this?"

"The only number unsaved."

"Oh so I guess you know me still," she asked, knowing it was Danny. She slid a hand down into her vagina. It was still tender.

"I could never forget my first lover and abandoner."

"Oh wow...so that's the reason you called?" she asked surprised, and irritated at the same time.

"Nawl, look. I got something I need to handle today. So tomorrow I'ma hit you up, and we can set up a meeting place and time."

Smiling at how deep his voice sounded, and how about his business he seemed, Alexis said, "Oh, well okay," as she fingered herself, slowly. "What you doing?" She was trying to turn the conversation toward another topic.

"Sitting here with my girl about to watch some dog conditioning videos, blow some sticky. Pop some skittles, sip some Black Henny."

Hearing that kind of crashed her hopes of getting a quick nut off, but she wasn't about to let it show. She removed her wet fingers from her centerpiece, and said "Oh, okay. That's what's up…hold on." Then after pausing, she said, "Danny, I'ma call you back, this an important call."

Danny started laughing, "You still do that. I guess old habits die slow."

"Danny, what you talkin' about?" she asked, twisting up her lips.

"Nothing, but yeah doe, I'ma hit you later."

When she heard the beep, she couldn't believe he hung up.

"Oh this niggroo got me fucked up," she said sending him a text, telling him how disrespectful he was.

His return text came back saying "I thought you had an important call," with a smiling face at the end of the text. Seeing the yellow smiley face, and sending him one in return, she knew, and felt there was still love in his heart for her.

Getting up, bored, Alexis decided to go shopping. Having seen a pair of BCBG Jeans, with a matching T-shirt, she knew she had to have it. She dressed and headed to the mall.

*****

As she swiped a Visa, she looked at her ring and felt wrong. Seeing her phone ringing, she answered it after gathering her shopping bags. "Hello," she answered.

"What's up shorty? What you got up?" asked Chino.

"Right now I'm buying me some cute panties and bras," she cooed, playing with his head.

"Oh yeah. Lace, thong, string, what kind?"

"None of your business! That's why it's Victoria's Secret," she joked.

"Aww, you no fun. But look. What mall you at? I'm trying to slide on you for a minute."

Thinking about what she told Stephon, she figured this meeting up with Chino would be perfect.

"I'm at the Frontnate," she told him.

"I'm on my way. I'm like twenty minutes away."

After ending the call, Alexis texted Stephon with, "Baby I love you. Be safe. And I'm doing my homework."

*****

"Aye, I got to make a quick stop real fast, alright?" said Chino, after getting off the phone. He and Alexis had been together damn near all day and he had yet to make a sale. But when one of his soldiers called saying they needed two more jars of pills, and a half a brick, he was on it.

"I ain't trippin' Chino, I know how the game go," Alexis stated. "Get yo' money."

Even though Alexis had that sparkling rock on her finger saying she was taken, her actions screamed 'Single.'

Whipping the Range Rover up the driveway of one of his stash houses, Chino parked in the garage, then shot inside. As he weighed the work, and stuffed it in a backpack, his phone started ringing. He wasn't about to answer the call until he noticed it was Alexis. "Shorty, what's up? I'm on my way out now," he told her almost releasing his pit bull from the basement.

"Oh I was about to ask if I could come in for a second. I gotta use the bathroom."

Not missing the chance of having her inside the house, he said "okay."

Letting Alexis in, she did the pee-pee dance while he locked the door back.

"Come on boy, you taking yo' slow time. Where the bathroom?" she asked with urgency.

"Down the hall, last door on the right." With that, she shot off down the hallway.

Getting at text from his soldier asking about the work, he texted back saying "On my way." Next Chino went to the bathroom door, "Lex I got to bust this move. I'll be back in a sec, alright?"

"Okay but don't be gone long, you know I got a curfew," she reminded him. She had a man to get home to.

"Yeah I know."

After dropping the work off, Chino stopped to get a fifth of white Remy, and some Swishers. Then instead of going straight back he drove a circular pathway in order to check on two of his trap houses. Both appeared to be jumping as he drove by. He knew Lex would be mad, but a few shots and a fat blunt of Sour

143

Diesel had a way of calming a bitch's nerves, he thought walking inside. She was hot, sitting on the sofa, legs crossed, arms folded with a mug.

"Don't be mad at me boo, I just had to check on a couple things." After rolling up, he poured her a glass. He sparked the weed and asked, "How's life really been treating you since you been out?"

"Well, I can't complain. I've been doing okay since I been home."

Chino passed her the blunt, "Oh yeah, speakin' of home, what joint was you at, and why you never hit me up?"

"I was in Greenville, Illinois. And I didn't risk calling because I didn't want the feds snooping into who I was in contact with. That's how niggas get knocked off all the time."

She blew the smoke out, then took a sip, confident that her reply would lower his guards completely. When she kicked her pumps off, and rested her legs across his lap, he knew she was feeling herself. Massaging her small feet and her calves, she started purring. That's when Chino kissed her French manicured toes, one by one.

"Owweee, that feels good. I see you still know how to touch my body."

"I still know how to do a lot of things to your body, all you got to do is let loose and give me the command." He started making a soft sensual trail of kisses up her leg. Alexis could feel her pussy pulsating with desire, but before she could say anything her phone was ringing.

"Hey babe...umm I'm leaving my friend Erica's house now. Yeah, I'll be there in less than an hour. Okay. I will. Love you too."

"Is there a problem?" asked Chino, already knowing what was going on.

"Arr! Yeah, I got to go. Take me to my car."

As they rode in silence, smoking, Chino kept looking over at her. Alexis looked pissed in the worst way, so when they got to her vehicle, he spoke up. "Shorty it seems like you ain't happy."

"And what makes you say that?"

"It's just a hunch...if you ain't you playin', cause you need to be."

"Yeah I hear what you saying Chino, but it's not that easy. This man held me down while I was locked away."

"So, what that mean, baby girl, you deserve to be happy, period!"

"Chino, please...don't make this hard on me."

"I'm not. But you is shorty. Just hit me when you need to smile and have a good time. You need anything, you get at me."

With a gleaming bright smile, Alexis said "I will." She reached over, kissed him on the cheek, then got in her Lexus. He sat there watching her pull off into night time traffic. With a grin, Chino knew in time, he was going to be back laying pipe to Alexis– married or not.

Chapter 19

While on her cell phone with her father, they scheduled the match, and set the weight of the dogs at 37-pounds. At the same time, both wired twenty-grand each to a mutual person in case of a forfeit, prior to the match.

"Daddy, I can't believe I'm betting against Tina Marie, you must think I'm crazy?"

Laughing, her father said, "I taught you well. There's obviously something you see in MaMa. Or Tina Marie. I've got a two-time champion stud waiting for her out in San Diego. I should be able to get 15-grand a pup, maybe more."

"Well Daddy, I'll see you in Fort Wayne for the fight in eight weeks. I love you," expressed Monica.

"I'm proud of you sweetheart. I'm going to email and text all my dog men across the country about the match. You do the same. I love you too."

Monica looked at her watch, worried about Danny's whereabouts. She texted him but got no reply.

*****

Knifing her way through traffic en route to make a sale, Becky purposely set the buy up to take place on one of Chino's blocks.Seeing his truck, and her customer in the same proximity, she looked to her right and asked Danny "Is you ready?"

"I came out the womb ready." Danny chambered a round into the H&K resting on his lap.

When the college girl walked up to Becky's truck, she said "Hey Becky, you got that for me?"

"Yeah. Here," she handed her a leather Coach purse. "Keep the bag. It's a gift for always shopping with me."

The young woman handed Becky the cash, smiling at the bag as she walked to her car not far away.Becky wasn't tripping on the bag, it was a gift Chino had given her a while back. But her heart raced, seeing Chino in full stride walking up.

"So that's where we at? You gone try me on my strip, bitch?" He rattled at her door latch, trying to open her truck door! It was locked.

"Boy, this ain't your strip! I can make money anywhere."

"Oh yeah. So now you gangsta?" questioned Chino as his soldier eased out his truck clutching a firearm.

"Nawl, she ain't. But I am!" barked Danny jumping out the backseat of Becky's truck. Once Chino and his street soldier saw Danny and the chopper their hands went up, and they started a slow back-peddle.

Becky stepped out into the night, "I see you ain't tough now Chino! This gotdamn block belongs to us now, either of you fuck boys got a problem with that?" asked Becky, smirking beneath a flickering street light.

"Nawl, Becky. You got that, for now."

"Good, now you and your little yes-man can go now."

As Chino and his soldier climbed up into his truck, and was about to pull off, his soldier leaned out the windows with his Glock! Boc! Boc! Boc!

Becky ducked, nearly falling to the ground as her driver's-side window shattered.

"Fuck you doin'?" yelled Chino, yanking him back into the Range Rover's cabin. But it was far too late, and Chino knew it.

Danny had already let his H&K rip holes through Chino's truck. Becky jumped inside her G-Wagon, seeing Chino's soldier dangling lifeless out the window. Chino recklessly swerved, avoiding an oncoming vehicle, crashing into a light pole! Meanwhile the two holes in his soldier's head painted the block crimson red. Leaving behind brass shell-casings all over the street, and shattered glass, Becky and Danny sped off.

Back at home, Becky was full of energy. She didn't really feel it was going to go down like that, but witnessing Danny put in work for her just turned her on.

"I can't believe we just did that! Oh my God, did you see his face?"

"Yeah, I saw his face. I tried to put a bullet in it, I fuckin' missed. You know this is only the beginning, right?" acknowledged Danny, considering retaliation.

"Yeah, but who cares... fuck Chino!" declared Becky, popping open a cold bottle of Ace of Spade. Passing Danny two ecstasy pills with Christmas trees on them, he turned them down. Danny's mind was everywhere. He glanced down at his watch, then he

149

observed Becky as she threw back three Naked Ladies. Then she took a long swig from the bottle.

"You might want to take those. I'm not taking you home no time soon. And I refuse to be told no."

Throwing the pills in his mouth, snatching the bottle, he washed them down. "Alright. But just know this ain't no lovey-dovey shit. You wanna fuck then that's what we gone do," he slurred, taking another swig.

Feeling like a queen on a chessboard, Becky said. "Okay. Bring it on then."

*****

Alexis had been sitting on the edge of the bathroom tub for nearly 45- minutes. Over the past couple weeks she'd felt bloated, although she wasn't on her period. Not only that, her appetite was voracious lately.So she decided to get a few pregnancy tests just to make sure she wasn't eating for two.

Now, she was waiting on her third test to come back, she put her face in her hands and was startled by the beep-beep-beeeep sound of the timer going off. She examined the digital display on the reading stick, and it came back 'positive' just like the last two. Exhaling, overcome with emotions of uncertainty, she sent Stephon a text telling him they needed to talk "ASAP!"

After getting a pint of Cookies 'N' Cream ice cream out of the deep freezer she turned on the local news, where a newscaster was talking about an overnight homicide. Alexis didn't know how Stephon was going to respond to the idea of a new baby, hell she was still in a state of denial her damn self.

150

"Ma, Alexis, where you at baby?" called Stephon, rushing into the house.

"I'm in the living room bae," she called out.

Walking into the living room, he noticed her balled up beneath a comforter. Sitting beside her on the edge of the sofa he asked. "What's wrong?"

"Baby, I'm gettin' fat ain't I?"

Looking confused, Stephon didn't know what to say in reply to her question.

"No, you're not fat...I mean you getting thicker but not fat, that's just because I been giving you good sex, and feeding you right. What's wrong doe Lexy?"

Sitting up, giving him direct eye contact she told him what it was, and his first response was, "Where the test at then?"

"Really," she said. Then she pointed toward the bathroom. "They in there."

As Stephon headed toward the bathroom, Alexis rolled over, pulling the comforter over her head. But before she knew it he came diving on the couch, tickling her. She tried to tell him to "turn me loose!" but that order fell on deaf ears.

"Ma, we gone have a baby!" he said, kissing her stomach.

While giggling, she said "Yeah, we is. So what you want to have?" Waiting for his answer, she rubbed her hand around his neck, ears, then through his wavy hair.

"I'm thinking a beautiful lil girl. What about you?" He rested his head on her stomach, feeling the bliss of a bond between man, woman, and child. The thought of being a better father than his dad was to him crossed his mind. He knew he would have to turn his robbery game up a few more notches in order to give the baby all it could ever dream of.

"Did you hear what I just said?" Alexis shook his shoulder, pulling him out of his daydream. "I said, it don't matter, as long as the baby healthy," she repeated.

"I love you Alexis," he assured her.

"I love you too," she cooed. "Now, come and dig inside your garden of love." She gripped his crotch, stroking his member until it was solid hard.

During their lovemaking Alexis had climaxed harder that she had in months, realizing that she was a bonafide squirter, and a creamer too.

When Alexis got up the next morning, she went to the walk-in clinic for a proper confirmation. She was right at 9-weeks along. And as a couple they couldn't have been happier. To them both the baby was the greatest gift from God.

She jumped when she heard his ringtone: "Say round, let me hit you right back, it's hot right na, the feds got my phone tapped." Hearing that sent Alexis from being the sweetest angel, to the devil's mistress, and with Stephon answering, it didn't help any either.

"What's the deal, Unc? Oh yeah? I'm with Lex right now," he said, cutting his eye at her. He started speaking in Spanish, then hung up.

"You know you're starting to get on my bad side," she yelled.

"What ma?"

"For one, did you forget, I do speak Spanish too dumb ass! So you got to find a way to get rid of me, huh?" She repeated, translating into English what he'd stated in Spanish.

"Bae, it's not like that."

"Well, how is it? You know what, I don't even care! It's crazy because we just found out we're going to have a baby, and you still want to run the streets fuckin' hoes, and robbing."

"Where's this coming from? Ain't nobody fucking hoes, how...stop—"

"Stephon please don't sit up here and lie, I'm not stupid. And ya little girl-friend texted you this morning too. You know what, just drop me off at my Aunt Rosie's house so you can go do you!"

At times, Alexis wanted to step out and cheat on Stephon, but she couldn't bring herself to do it. It surely wasn't because he was faithful, because she knew he wasn't. It felt mainly due to her undefined love she had for him. Being there for her during them lonely days in prison meant the world to Alexis.

Pulling up at her aunt's house, before she could hop out of the car, he grabbed her arm. "Listen to me, Alexis, I love you. And nothing will ever change that. I'm sorry that I live the life that I live but this is who I am, and I promise in time it will get better."

As much as she didn't believe a word Stephon said, her heart did. Leaning over she kissed him. "I love you baby. Be safe," was all she could say.

"I love you too."

Chapter 20

Chino couldn't phantom the stunt Becky and her little Chicano had pulled last night. He let the whole scene rewind in his mind. He knew in his heart he'd cheated death, and frowned that his soldier wasn't as fortunate.

Having put all of his traps on high alert, Chino had just delivered some serious artillery to his guys. Unsure of what all plans Becky had up her sleeve, Chino found himself now in a rental seeking her out for vengeance. War had been declared.

Seeing De'Audie's number ringing his phone, Chino really didn't want to answer, but since this was his plug he picked it up.

"Whud up?"

"I'ma hearing you're having you self a little problem?"

"Nawl," he mumbled. "Where you gettin' your intel from? I don't have problems, I'm a problem solver." Chino held the line, wondering how De'Audie knew about his beef with the Crips.

"Thee person you're having a disagreement with is...how should I say?...is family."

Listen, I don't know what or who you're talking about. Maybe you should make it a little clearer," stated Chino getting frustrated.

"Becky. She works for someone special to me and it's best for all involved to end y'all disagreement."

"What!? How you know? Man, fuck her, and her little boyfriend drilled one of my guys last night." Chino was furious, realizing Becky was plugged.

"Ah yess I heard about this. But wasn't it you who threw the first stone? For the sake of getting to thee money, count it as a favor to me."

"Yeah, whatever you say boss," stated Chino sarcastically. He didn't care what De'Audie was saying. He was going to deal with Becky and her dude. And as if De'Audie could read his mind he spoke on it.

"It would be a shame for you to give me your word, and go back on it. Us as Shottas, all we have is our word, and for a man to dishonor his word is betrayal. Death is the promised reward for betrayal. You understand me?"

"Yeah, understood. I'ma leave Becky be."

"Good, and I will be hoping to see you as always in a week, yes?"

"Yeah, but aye, I got a move to shoot."

"Understood...be safe my friend," said De'Audie.

Disconnecting with De'Audie, Chino punched the steering wheel of his rental. After lighting up a blunt, he rode around checking his traps. He was searching his brain trying to figure out why dude that Becky was with looked so familiar to him.

Stopping by LA's house, Chino noticed him pulling his F-150 out into the street. He got out and greeted him. "Love folks, where you headed?"

156

"Kane got a big match tonight, you should slide with me."

Chino smiled, "Oh yeah, bet. Shit I definitely need to make some easy cash."

Kane was a brawling 2-time grand champion of Jeep and Niggarina blood. Everytime he got in the box he fought till the death. He didn't have a gram of fat on his body, just muscle, a big heart and old war wounds.

Kane's nose was tilted upward, as he smelled the stench of dog blood in the air.

Chino caught a $5,000 side bet with some white boys from Alabama who seemed serious about tonight's action. The place as overflowing with dog men and their women and even some kids. Chino loved dogs but wasn't the type to invest in the blood sport.

All he wanted was a fearless dog that would protect his stash houses. He began to watch the fight, as he started thinking of finding a suitable female pitbull for Four to enjoy. He was five and had yet to get any pussy, Chino thought. This event took Chino's mind off of everything that had been going wrong in the streets. As he watched Kane do battle he knew it wouldn't be much longer. LA was in a corner, watching his beast, chanting "Kill em, Kane!" and Kane was doing just that.

All of a sudden, that familiar face came into Chino's view. It was him. "What a small world," Chino whispered to no one at all. He intently scanned the crowd, figuring he would see Becky with him. But instead a young sexy Latina with a clipboard sat right beside him. Her shirt said "Ecstasy Kennels" in bold letters. Chino observed as the two of them enjoyed the fight. The girl was doing a scouting report or something.

"I'm about to clap this nigga's head off!" Having been forced to by the law of the sport, Chino had left his pistol in the truck. His mind raced for a plan of action. Knowing the truck was locked, the only option would be to pick up a brick and shatter the window.A few hundred-dollars would replace it. LA would understand.

By the time Chino found a brick and was cocking his arm like Tom Brady, a never-ending crowd began to pour out of the barn that had been converted into a mini stadium. Some people were sad, some were happy. "Who won that last match?" Chino asked a white couple.

"Kane killed the other dog."

Hearing that Chino raced back inside, not seeing Danny, and not seeing the people he'd bet! "Fuck! Fuck! Fuck!!" he screamed.

When LA came out, he had Kane in a small kennel. He hoisted the dog into the bed of the truck. Although he'd won close to 20-grand, he didn't seem happy. "I gotta get my man Kane home. He lost an eye, and a whole lot of blood." LA wiped away a tear.

"But he wouldn't stop scratching till he killed his opponent. I love that dog folks, straight up."

Chino threw up his pitch forks, "DO OR DIE KENNELS my nigga."

*****

Having endless ecstasy pills, walking the runway, and photo shoots constantly had changed Becky in a drastic way. She had just finished a magazine cover photo shoot for Kite magazine up in Brooklyn, New York and was on her way to meet up with Deeiaz.

Ever since she confided in Deeiaz about her situation with Chino, Deeiaz was keeping a close eye on her. She was offered a personal bodyguard, and assigned a driver as well.

Now today, Becky was told that after her photo shoot she was to fly back to St. Louis for an important meeting. She did as told and hoped for the best. She couldn't see going back to the lame lifestyle she lived before meeting Deeiaz.

When the 'Boo Thang' ringtone started playing on her cellphone she smiled, knowing it was Danny. Becky had really grown strong feelings for him. And even though he had a girl at home, she still wanted him.

"And I'm going to get you," she declared to herself before answering.

"Hey boo, what's up?"

"Shit, man, just getting back to the D. Where you at?"

"On my way to a meeting, I'm just getting back from a photo shoot up in New York. I'm gonna be on the cover of Kite magazine, and maybe even Snowflakes magazine too."

"Oh yeah, that's what's up. Aye so I seen your lil friend the other day."

"Baby, my lil friend right here in my purse. It's black and loud and holds 16 slugs," joked Becky, groping around in her Berkin bag feeling her cold steel.

"I'm talking about Chino. He was out in the country cornfields at a dog show. He didn't know I seen him. If my girl wasn't with me I woulda sent him to exist amongst the angels, you feel me?"

"You don't have to worry about him. I've already taken care of that situation, so you good."

"I'm good, I ain't worried about me. I'm worried about you. You the one still be making moves in the city," stated Danny. He was now cruising up Gratiot, feeling good to be back. His goals were to spend the next two months conditioning Ma-Ma for her upcoming match, and booming the biggest load of pills he'd gotten from Becky at one time.

"Awww, you worried about me. That's cute."

"Yeah shorty. Just be safe okay, I'ma hit you later."

"Alright. Boo I will. You do the same."

When Becky hung up, her heart just fluttered at the idea of him being worried about her. That geeked her head up even more that she was really a somebody.

Pulling up to a beautiful Jamaican restaurant, Becky's driver parked at the back door. When it opened, three heavily-armed men stepped out carrying assault rifles with Mickey Mouse drums. Next a lady who was sophisticated and well-dressed opened the car door.

"Mrs. and Mr. Benjamin are waiting for you," said the lady as she helped Becky out of the truck, then she escorted her into the building. As they got closer to the designated meeting area, Becky saw more and more men and women armed with military-style weapons and combat gear.

Once they reached a huge marble double-door, the soft-spoken woman asked Becky if she wanted anything to eat.

"Umm yes. Can I have some baked fish, with a side of macaroni and cheese, some fresh broccoli, and a slice of strawberry cheesecake."

Smiling she said, "Your order will be ready in 30-45 minutes." She walked off.

The first face Becky saw was Chino's. That ruined what appetite she'd had. Seeing Deeiaz and Audie sitting at opposite ends of the long mahogany conference table was all the urging Becky needed to walk over, and seat herself closer to Deeiaz.

"Becky I'm so happy you were able to make it in once piece," stated Deeiaz standing up, giving her a hug and a kiss on both cheeks.

What the fuck is he doing here, Becky was thinking, "Yeah me too." She pointed over at Chino. "Why is he here? That's the ass I was telling you about!"

"Yes. I know. And that is why we are all here today. It seems you two have truly gotten off on the wrong foot."

Chino stood up, "Ain't no wrong foot but the foot I'ma put in that bitch ass. Shorty cold disrespected me on my block, and her people killed one of my guys!" growled Chino.

"That's what he deserved for shooting at me. Danny was only protecting me," said Becky, turning red.

"Understandable, but at the end of thee day blood was shed, so now in order to keep business afloat, and everyone safe and happy, how as a family, do we handle this?" asked Audie, puffing on a Cuban cigar.

"Me personally," Chino pounded the table, "will call it even when 'Danny' meets the same fate!"

"Over my dead body!" shouted Becky.

"How about one-hundred thousand dollars?" suggested Audie. "That should be enough for a proper burial," he added.

"I can't lay a price on the head of one of my soldiers. His life meant something to me."

"If it meant so much you should've had him trained."

"Bitch watch your mouth!" yelled Chino making his way toward Becky, but one of the armed guards pointed his rifle at him, placing a red beam dead in the center of his chest.

"I don't know you, and really don't care if you live or die, yet if you care for your own life, I would suggest you sit down, and never use that degrading word in front of me again!" yelled Deeiaz.

Chino sat back in his chair, cutting his eyes from Becky, to Deeiaz, then back to the armed guards. Becky couldn't help but smirk, but Chino's next move is what surprised her.

"Alright, one-hunned grand. And when shall I be expecting this payment?"

"When this meeting is over," Deeiaz assured him.

Becky was lost in her thoughts. She had never seen or known Chino to agree to someone else's terms, but then again, he didn't have the upper hand either. During the rest of the meeting they discussed plans of opening up rave clubs in St. Louis, Chicago, Miami and Atlanta. Chino used that as an opportunity to ask Audie about ways of getting a more reliable cocaine connection.

The cost of kilos had gone up from 18 to 29 thousand within three years.

"Well, until the Mexican cartels end their ongoing war, Chino, prices will continue to rise. But I will certainly look into it."

Becky's mind was on Chino's easy submission. She figured she knew him all too well. Hell, at one point in her life she was deeply in love with him. Once the meeting was over, she walked up to Chino and expressed that she was sorry for the loss of his friend.

"It's all good. Plus, a hunnid-grand will make sure he didn't die in vain," he replied. Just those words alone, and the shit-eating grin on Chino's face let her know that her gut feelings were right. So with that, she casually pulled down her Chanel sunglasses over her face and climbed up into the backseat of the Benz.

"Where to my lady?" asked the driver.

"Just drive around downtown, I need to think." She sat there, gazing off in traffic.

In the game she was in, Becky learned that nothing was to be taken for what it was on the surface. There was always a deeper meaning; a trick to the trade. So now, she was trying to figure out where, and what the trick was. As they rode around the city, the only thing that kept coming to mind was Danny. And the more he kept coming to mind the more she worried.

"I guess in time all will be revealed," she admitted to herself, then next she poured a cup of Ace of Spades.

"Driver," called Becky. "Take me to the mall, I feel like doing some shopping."

"Yes, my lady."

Chapter 21

You could barely see Uncle Harold's big black hand clutching his cell as he yelled into it at Danny, "What the fuck you mean you can't do it?"

"Just what I said Unc," Danny told him, "I'm not no ATM machine."

"Shit, I can't tell, how you be blowing all that money on Ma-Ma. Is you losing your mind?"

"You wanna make some money Unc, you need to bet with us. Ma-Ma is that bitch!"

"I'd never bet against Tina Marie, don't be like me and go down that road. Monica should know better. But anyway, look, I'm caring for your eight dogs down here. That costs. Using my staff. That costs. Taxes on the land, costs! I need five racks a fuckin' month nigga. You know what it is."

Danny was heated by some of the snide comments his uncle had made. It was like ever since he'd given him that bankroll the night he'd met up with Becky, Harold had been laying a soft press on him.

"Hey, I take the risk and I hustle in order to have money to blow, and you right. You down there caring for my dogs. I was

165

planning on hitting your hand, but I might wind up hitting you in the eye, nigga," said Danny.

"Lil nigga, half-breed ass nigga, you better watch your mouth and remember who the fuck I am," barked Harold.

"That's how you feel Unc? You acting like we ain't blood."

"Listen, I'm going to Western Union in an hour, I need to be picking up about 10 bands, or else the past is gonna haunt your stupid...betting against Tina Marie's ass!"

The more Uncle Harold tried using extortion tactics by bringing up the past, the more the pit of Danny's stomach turned. Danny had come to a point that he hated parasite ass niggas. Harold was turning into a leech, and he knew too much.

As Danny sat in his living room incensed, counting out the ten-grand he planned to have Monica wire Uncle Harold, a few things came to mind. It was as if everybody he dealt with always had something extra with them. It never failed; Becky wanting him to herself, Monica had been wanting him to invest in her beauty salon idea, and now, Uncle Harold. Everybody always wanted something; everybody but Alexis.

As he thought about her, realizing he didn't make time for her while in St. Louis, he decided to give her a call.

"Hello, who is this?" she asked sleepily.

"Danny, what you doing?"

"Umm, nothing, at my aunt's just getting up."

"I wanted to let you know, I apologize for not getting at you when I was that way. I had a lot going on. I'm—"

"You full of shit," said Alexis.

"Listen, stop playing like we cool or even on good terms. You left me after what happen, so you don't fuck with me. If you did you wouldn't be marrying somebody else. You wouldn't have been fuckin' Chino."

Alexis took a deep breath, listening to Danny's maturity and perspective. For some reason, a tear trickled down her face. "Danny, you remember that night when... what you done?"

"Yeah, what about it?"

"I promise you, I didn't know how to deal with it. I mean everything that went down, I felt, and still feel. It was my fault. Especially the kid," she cried. "I figured if I just distanced myself from you it would all go away. But it didn't. Then as if I was being punished by a higher power, I got locked up. And you wouldn't answer my calls. I was so lonely and lost."

"How you think I felt and I'm the one that did it?" asked Danny. "I have nightmares to this day."

"Danny, I've got to get ready for church, I love you."

"Hello? Hello?"

Realizing that Alexis had hung up, Danny ate two ecstasy pills, rolled a blunt and threw on his Timberlands. Next he went out to see Ma-Ma who was around back, running circles, and snatching her heavy duty chain, jumping up, excited to see Danny. All of the dogs were barking, wagging their tails. Danny had checked out some blogs, and the bets on the Tina Marie/Ma-Ma match were skyrocketing.

While walking Ma-Ma till her tongue dangled out her mouth, gave Danny time to reflect on everything going on in his life, and all he'd been through. He smiled as he recalled the night he aired

167

Sugar Man out. Even though he smoked the kid, he had no regrets. This was the life he chose to live and living it to the fullest was a must, not an option.

After putting Ma-Ma in a clean kennel, with fresh straw bedding, Danny fed her a prescribed portion of raw chicken breasts, and oatmeal. Next, as he took Forbidden off his chain Monica came out of the house. "Uncle Harold's blowin' my cell phone up. Were you supposed to send him something?"

*****

Chino was holding a 40 ounce outside of one of his trap houses as a group of his street soldiers were all shooting dice. For a Sunday afternoon, the trap was jumping. He had just gotten off the phone with a funeral home up Chicago and was about to bury their comrade. It was the least he could do.

One guy yelled, "I got fifty you don't six-eight, folks!"

Another chimed in with "I got a hunn-do you don't six."

They all dropped their cash on the ground and waited for the man to roll the dice. Instead of rolling them, he stood there shaking them in his hand, them put his hand—still shaking the dice up to his ear, "I like to listen to 'em before I shoot 'em." He flicked his wrist sending the dice out spinning.

Landing on two fours, he yelled "Bet back!" and scooped up a couple bills, as the dude dropped another few bills. The guy shook the dice again, snapping his fingers as the dice spun from his fingertips, finally falling on a six and two. The group all started laughing and yelling. Chino was simply observing it all. He was geeked off ecstasy he'd taken. He watched the man who was now blowing on the hot dice before shooting. The dice stopped on five and one. The guy yelled "Nationwide, point seen. Don't nobody move but the shooter!"

Two ladies walking up the block who were thicker than a Snicker caught Chino's attention. One was in a pair of leggings and Jordans, while the shorter and thicker of the two wore a pair of red booty shorts. When the chicks looked back, that's when Chino and two of his soldiers made their move. Pulling one of the young girls to the side, Chino laid his mack down while the other two guys seduced the shorter one.

Whispering in her ear, trying to get shorty to come inside the house with him created a distraction because only one out of the group of men peeped the slow-cruising Caravan heading their way. "Folks, watch out!" one of the youngest soldiers on the porch yelled, alerting them all to the imminent danger. Looking up, getting low, Chino saw the three Crips hopping out, donning blue rags, concealing their identities. More disturbing was the Mac 10s in their hands spitting fire!

"Oh shit!" yelled Chino, snatching the screaming lady up he'd been talking to like a shield, as he trampled behind his rental car with her. He slung her to the pavement.

"Please let me go! Oh my god!"

"Shut up bitch!" growled Chino.

Still holding her down, Chino pushed her completely underneath the vehicle and peeked over the hood. As soon as the shooting began, he had wrestled out his P89. What he thought was just three dudes, turned out to be four, and they had cut down his two soldiers and the other chick. But the shooting didn't stop! As his anger started boiling from watching his men dropping to the pavement, he lost all perception and tact. Cracking open the door of the rental, just enough to get his hands on the AR-15 laying in the backseat, he chambered a round! Then rose to his feet, "GD bitches!" Boom! Boom! Boom! Squeezing the trigger sent the closest two Crips straight to hell, as one took cover behind a nearby tree. The third turned into easy prey when his gun jammed up. He dropped it, taking off running!

Boom! The headshot didn't take but a nanosecond to send his skull splattering into a thousand different directions all at once, followed by his near-decapitated body crashing into a parked Buick.

It was a horrific scene. Several of Chino's men struggled for dear life, crawling with tattered, blood-soaked clothes. All of them clutching at least one of the bullet holes in their torsos or legs. That's when the assassin behind the tree took her sweet time, releasing the empty 30-round clip, slamming in a loaded one. The metallic steel sliding against steel sound of a round being chambered caught Chino by surprise, but the very bullet and sixteen more that followed ended his life! As Chino laid there spread-eagled, convulsing, letting out a nasty 10-second death rattle, coughing up blood, the girl crying beside him begged God for help. On her knees, she crawled through Chino's pool of blood and mangled flesh and escaped with her life.

The shooter, dressed in blue, ran to the waiting van, only after stumbling to the ground dropping the gun. Down a busy street the van disappeared in traffic.

Chapter 22

After she'd jogged for an hour straight on a custom-designed treadmill, Monica unhooked Ma-Ma, and immediately checked her heart rate using a digital sensor. The beast couldn't help herself, she gave Monica wet kisses until the display lit up. Monica jotted down the number on a clipboard and took Ma-Ma to her water bowl. Next she weighed her. She was a muscular 39 pounds, still 2 pounds overweight.

Monica had been up majority of the night watching videos of Tina Marie's past matches. She knew her strengths and weaknesses. So with knowing her opponent's tendencies, she wanted to train Ma-Ma in a way that she'd naturally fight in a certain way that exploited Tina Marie's weaknesses. Finding a sparring mate that fought similar to Tina's style was the order of the day.

Just as Monica connected Ma-Ma to a weighted pulling sled, Danny came into the training area with some upsetting news, "Monica, I need to talk with you baby girl, it's important."

He knelt down beside her and Ma-Ma as Forbidden cried and barked in the distance for Danny's care and attention. "Check it, I was over at my man Boog's but I left after setting up a match involving Forbidden right. It's some 7 Mile niggas claiming they got a killa, and a quarter ticket to put on him," he said running out of breath.

"Slow down," Monica told him, really beginning to worry. Her intuition was on full alert.

"So, I leave Boog's, on my way to see Frankie over at the club, I see ATF, DEA, FBI and the local cops leaving out the club, of course I keep it pushing. Before I could even get home, I get a call from the federal U.S. Attorney who prosecutes cases for this district telling me he's got an arrest warrant for a criminal complaint that's been filed here, plus one down in St. Louis! Wants me to turn myself in!"

*****

When Alexis found out Chino was a dead man she was crushed. Local news was reporting that one of the suspects they were looking for was a woman named Melissa Brown. Her fingerprints were all over the gun that murdered Chino. The authorities felt she was now in Marietta, Georgia, and that they had a "relationship dispute."

This was a huge game changer with Chino dead, Alexis began to rub her belly, considering how to locate more of Chino's stash houses. She'd only been to one of them.

Stephon was still robbing, and doing more of it seeing the baby would be demanding of more income. Alexis was going to get a job and set up the perfect heist for Stephon. What he was now doing needed to come to an end. More than anything, she wanted her child growing up with a father in her life, unlike her childhood.

In order to stick with the script, Alexis had to attend Chino's funeral up in Chicago. So after that she sent a few texts, and got on Facebook and Instagram, finding out that LA was next in line to receive the honor of Chino's crown, which made it all the sweeter.

On the drive back from Chicago, she recalled the first time she'd met LA. She was over Chino's getting a half a bird. But when Chino walked off LA was drooling over her, begging her to let him pay to play.

"I guess you just might get your chance," she mumbled to herself, calling him up. She was eager to see how he was taking Chino's passing.

"I'm cool, just fucked up my dog gone. What's up with you doe?"

"Yeah, I know right, that shit crazy. I'm lonely, on my way home, just thinking about all the good times," she said, tossing the worm out. And like a hungry fish, he grabbed it.

"You ain't got to be lonely right now."

"Huh, what you mean?" she asked, playing dumb.

"I'm sayin'. We can keep each other company. You feel me?"

"I feel you. Mmmmhm. But where we gone meet at?"

After a pause, he suggested they meet up at the house on MLK.

"I thought that was Chino's place, I'm like...not trying to be at his spot with...you."

"Nawl, that's our spot, he just kept the demonstration there," LA corrected her, trying to persuade her, but at the same time running his mouth a little too much.

"I've been driving for hours, let me shower, get dressed. Is 45-minutes okay?"

"Alright, see you then."

Alexis showered up at her aunt's, putting on Victoria's Secret Sour Apple lotion, and a cute revealing sundress and she was in motion with her plan. As she thought about her daughter, and the unborn child she was carrying, she figured this would be the easiest and safest way to provide a good start for her family. Selling drugs she would never do again. Before getting out her car, she texted LA, letting him know she was outside. By the time she made it to the front door it was open, and he was there ushering her inside.

"Damn, baby girl, you'll be dropping that bundle of joy soon, huh?" he said with a warm smile.

"This baby be having me hungry and horny all at the same time."

Sharing a laugh about her comment, he asked Alexis if she was hungry now.

"Umm," she giggled. "I am actually, but I bought me some snacks."

"Fuck no! If you are hungry I'ma cook you something to eat. What yall got a taste for?"

With a grin, she said "Chicken, or shrimp, no... Chicken and shrimps."

She watched as he strolled over to the TV and turned on some relaxing music, then headed for the kitchen. Following behind LA, she smiled as he pulled a bag of frozen chicken tenders, and jumbo shrimp from the deep freezer. As he started preparing the food he told her to "Get comfortable. I got some lambs fur house shoes in the back room so you can take them shoes off. I know them toes hurting."

"Okay playa," she said smiling. "I hear you."

He laughed.

"The next thing you'll be offering me is a foot rub," she said walking toward the back room.

"If that's what it takes, then it's done."

Going into the room she flipped her shoes off, and started snooping through dressers. Not finding anything, she slipped into the cozy house shoes and was making her way back until she noticed a bolt lock on the other bedroom door.

"Bingo!" she whispered, knowing the lock meant there was something of importance in that room.

Getting back to the living room, her stomach started growling when she smelled the food frying.

"Damn boy! You got it smelling soo good, like you know what you doing?"

"That's because I do," he said, picking up a strip of chicken, blowing on it, so it wouldn't be so hot. She bit it, and as she started chewing the flavor hit her taste buds, she moaned, "mmm, this so good."

"Yeah, what about this," he asked doing the same with a shrimp and feeding it to her.

Closing her eyes while chewing, she had to give her compliments to the chef. "Mm-m-mm, a man like you'd spoil me. Yeah, you did this, so when can I eat while you got me sampling it?" She smiled.

"It depends if you wanna wait for the sides or not."

"Fuck them sides, I'm hungry now!"

Both laughing at her candidness, he said, "Have it your way."

After he grabbed both trays, heading for the living room he told her to "Get the ranch dressing and hot sauce."

The more time Alexis spent with LA, the harder it was becoming for her to play her role. He was being a real gentleman.

"What's on your mind?" asked LA, bringing her out of her daydream.

"Nothing's wrong," she said, looking seductive. "I'm just wondering why you being so nice to me, and you see I'm fat." While rubbing on her stomach, she awaited his reply, batting her eyelashes. "You're not fat crazy girl, you're pregnant."

"Okay, that's even worse, why you being all sweet to another nigga baby mama?"

"Listen I'm not trying to replace dude, or be a second baby daddy to your baby. I'm just going after what I like and treating you how I feel you should be treated, that's all."

Looking in his eyes she saw he meant every word, and without thinking, she leaned over and kissed him. As their tongues started slow dancing, he softly guided her on his lap, filling both his palms with her soft ass, causing her to moan. Then she began to wind and grind on his large erection; much larger than she'd ever felt. Now ready to cut her wild side loose, she started unbuckling his belt and tugging at his pants, anxious to get her mouth around his mammoth-size dick. That's when Stephon's dedicated ringtone started playing. Jumping off his lap, she just stared at her purse, chewing on her nails. Overcome with the feeling of arousal, and then guilt for the act she was so willing and ready to commit. What am I doing? she asked herself.

"Is you going to answer that?" asked LA, nursing his erection with his hand.

Without a reply, she ran to the back room, put her shoes on, and with her head down, she returned back to the living room.

"LA, I have to go, I'm sorry!"

"Ain't nothing to be sorry about. All I ask is just be safe driving home and regret nothing."

Nodding her head, she ran out the house, and into her vehicle. Pulling off, before even buckling up, she was trying to put as many miles as she could between them. "What the hell is wrong with you!?" she screamed at herself, "How could you be so vulnerable!!"

When Stephon's ringtone went off she flinched, afraid to answer, fearing her husband-to-be knew what she'd done, but she answered anyway.

"Hey baby."

"What's up ma, you alright?" asked Stephon worriedly.

"Yeah, I'm fine. I was inside the store when you called, I had left my phone in the car," she lied.

"Oh yeah. When you start doing that, huh? But check it out. I know we've been on some bullshit terms lately because of my actions. So I been thinking, maybe we can go out on the town tonight, have some fun, and discuss you coming home. I miss my cuddle buddy."

Thrilled to be hearing the man she really loved trying to make amends brought about a smile. "Okay babe, meet me at the house, so we can get a round in before we go out."

*****

It was like even in death Chino was bringing Becky problems. She'd just found out he was dead, and now Deeiaz was interrogating her trying to determine if she had any involvement.

"Come on Deeiaz, you know that's not even my style."

"That's what I thought as well, until the last situation happened. They're reporting on the news that one of the shooters was a female by the name of Melissa. So you know her? Did you attend school with her, Becky?"

"As far as I know, she was Chino's main lady, his 'bottom bitch' is what he would call her. But I'd never met her in my life."

There was a muffling sound of Deeiaz covering up the receiver of the phone, relaying Becky's responses to someone else. Seeing the angle in which Deeiaz was probing, Becky then understood why she was a suspect.

"Okay," stated Deeiaz, returning to the phone. "So, like I said, Becky, we—"

"I can understand where you're coming from but that was squashed at our sit-down, so what's my motive, some street corner in St. Louis?" cried Becky, trying to get her supplier and friend to see her innocence.

"That's very much true, however, I truly hope you didn't have anything to do with it because it's going to be a sad celebration for those responsible."

With that being understood, Becky ended her call, and was hoping Danny had nothing to do with it. Knowing there was only one way to find out she dialed him up. That's when an automated recording played informing callers that the number was disconnected. Stressing now, she tried again, only to get the same result. She tried once more, "What the fuck!"

After pacing back and forth, Becky headed upstairs to her huge bedroom, but suddenly the walls started closing in on her, as she sat there on the edge of her bed, overwhelmed with worry. "What the hell's going on with Danny?" she whispered, after reaching for a partially smoked blunt laying in a night stand ashtray.

Seaching her list of contacts, she then discovered a secondary phone number Danny had once given her in case of an emergency. Becky smiled, then hit 'call'.

"Hello, Danny?"

"Nawl, this isn't Danny, and may I ask who this is?" asked a woman territorially.

Hearing the female's voice caused Becky to glance at her phone.

"Umm this is Becky. Danny and I do business together. Is he around, please?" asked Becky, in a humble way.

"Nawl, he ain't, and what type of business do yall do together, *Becky*?"

Hearing how the woman on the other end put emphasis on 'Becky', Becky knew it was meant to sound intimidating.

This has to be Danny's girlfriend, Becky thought, finally getting her chance of wedging her way in. "With all due respect, it's up to him to inform you on what all our business entails, that's if he puts his *trust* in you. But if you can, please tell him it's verrry important he gets up with me A-S-A-P. Thank You."

Hearing the 'beep,' Becky smiled, knowing she had managed to get under the girl's skin. Even though she knew Danny would likely be upset with her, she didn't care. In any event, Danny still had three-hundred and fifty-thousand dollars' worth of ecstasy pills that she'd given him on consignment. "I need my money, bullshit ain't nothing. Hmm."

After pouring herself a drink, she flicked on the news. They were still reporting about the fastly climbing murder rate in St. Louis. "It's a shame," said Becky gazing down at her pooch. Becky began to wonder what her life would be like if she'd been a lawyer, instead of her current occupation.

Seeing her phone was ringing, Becky turned the depressing TV off and answered, "Hello?"

"It's a sold out show, sweetheart," said a woman Becky knew to be her worker at a rave club, and often worked the pole too at a downtown strip club.

"Okay boo, I'll come see you around sevenish okay." Becky gazed at her Rolex, seeing it was six o'clock.

"That's cool. Do you think you can bring me some trees too?"

"I thought you quit smoking girl, what happen?"

"Girl I need more than some vodka to deal with these niggas and they tired ass game."

Both the ladies started giggling, then Becky told her "okay," and started undressing. In nothing but her birth suit, she looked at her jaw-droppin' figure in the full-length mirror. She turned around, looking over at her butt, wondering where she got it all from.

As Becky soaped up with a sponge, her hand brushed against her clit, sending her hormones beyond the moon. Remembering the promise she made to herself she yelled out "Boy you need to be calling me!" Thinking about Danny, he was the only person she wanted playing with her kitty, so she rushed out the shower before she broke her promise.

Squeezing into a skintight, python printed Donna Karen cat suit that fit her like a glove, she was off to her stash house. Pulling up to the home in her leased Bentley GT, the neighbors looked her up and down lustfully. She was known as an urban model to many, but only a few knew her as the plug. Some even said she was the one who had Chino whacked. With a rep like that people stayed out her way.

Climbing a pull-down ladder leading up into the attic, Becky grabbed a few ounces of weed, and a half-dozen jars of pills. As she was getting into her car, she noticed an all black Yukon bending the corner that sent chills through her body. Her initial thoughts said 'Police,' so when she pulled off she did it smooth, and slow. But when the Yukon blocked off the entire street, she saw an identical truck right on her rear bumper! Becky was feeling that something was foul, having never seen police execute this type of stop. That's when she witnessed the first black dude hop out bandannaed up, concealing his face, holding an AK-47. In an instant she thought the worst and mashed the gas to the floor! The Bentley's tires screeched!

As bullets ripped through the Bentley, Becky sent the first man out the truck flipping over the windshield. As her car jumped the curb, her rear window shattered, then fell completely out. "What the fuck! God please!" was all she could manage to scream while fishtailing around the corner, her tires screeching and smoking, she prayed it was over. Not seeing anymore flying bullets, nor hearing gunfire, she thought she was home free, until looking up into her rearview mirror. One of the two trucks was in hot pursuit, and a ski-masked man was hanging out the window taking aim, orange flames leaping from his stick. Seeing her dashboard shredding to bits as bullets struck, Becky screamed. Next, she felt her body jerk forward; one of the slugs catching her in the shoulder. This caused her to swerve, side-swiping two parked cars. Quickly gaining control, she punched the accelerator again, with only one arm of use. "Please God! I don't wanna die!" she cried out, blacking in and out of consciousness. Hearing 'Boo Thang' playing, she felt her savior was coming. With her left thumb she pressed the 'Answer Call' button on her steering wheel, "Danny! Help! Please baby help! Somebody's shootin' at me!"

Just then her headrest exploded in a cloud of leather, cotton and jagged pieces of metal fragments. Then a volley of bullets tore holes in the windshield!

"Becky! What's going on? Where you at Becky?"

As Danny called out her name, Becky's Bentley slammed into the corner of a house. Both black trucks crept by. After seeing her face bloody, head submerged in the white air bag the men retreated, feeling the job was completed.

Chapter 23

Life was really going from sugar to shit for Danny. First Frankie getting grabbed by the feds. Then the warrants in St. Louis and Detroit. Now he was trying frantically in his head to understand Becky's situation. By the time he turned his cell phone off, and made his way home he was met at the door with some more shit.

With a finger in his face Monica yelled, "Nigga, I'm done!"

"What is you talkin' about?" asked Danny.

"I'm talkin' about your white whore, Becky. That's what I'm talkin' about...so sick of everytime I look up it's a new bitch you dealing with."

Danny didn't know how she knew of Becky and it wasn't something worth denying. Plus he had more on his mind than to worry about some nonsense, so he just walked off, and started packing up.

Through the grapevine, Danny had learned today that Frankie was also in the heroin game, his indictment further said he was a major player in an international prostitution ring. And now that he was cased up, Danny was willing to step to the plate and gain ownership of the club, and its potential revenue. But first he had to figure out where the murder in the Lou came from. Was this

Sugar Man and them? he asked himself, looking at Monica's lips moving, but he couldn't hear a word she was saying. That was until she slapped the taste out his mouth! "So you don't have shit to say?" Her eyes proved she'd been crying.

"Say about what?" He rubbed the stinging sensation and walked around her, stuffing clothes into his duffle bag. "I don't know what the fuck to say because I don't know what you talking about."

"I'm talking about that bitch Becky calling this phone talking about it's important, and all ya'll business, and to call her A-S-A-P!"

Snatching the phone, he yelled "You answered my phone? Who told you to answer it?"

"It kept ringing so I thought it was important," she lied.

Danny headed into the bedroom, and dug out a backpack and threw it to Monica. She unbuckled it, looking inside, seeing rubber-banded stacks of cash. She asked, "What's this for?"

"For you to move on with your life. That's a little under a quarter-million. Do with it as you please."

With that said, Danny finished packing and was getting ready to disappear. He had to go back to St. Louis to see what was up with Becky.

"Really...that's it? Hell no, you and that bitch got me fucked up! So because she calls, you leaving?"

"Monica, you said you done! Well be done then. I got too much goin' on right now. So since you want out, you got it."

Feeling the coldness in his voice, seeing it in his eyes let Monica know he was serious, but she was lost. They had these types of fights all the time, so what made him decide to cross the 'It's over forever' threshold. What about the life they'd been building together, the dogs, Ecstasy Kennels, the huge upcoming dog match. Their future.

"Do you love her?" asked Monica.

"What? Are you for real?"

"Do you love her, damnit!?" she asked again, this time with tears rolling down her face.

"I love you," he told her.

"So why is you pushing me away then?"

"This what you said you wanted, so Monica, now you got it."

Danny started walking toward the front door, seeing this Monica slung the heavy bag at him, knocking him into the wall.

"I don't give a shit about this money! I come from money, Danny. All I wanted was for us to be happy, and for us to start a business, and for you to get out this life."

"Listen…just move on…any man would love a woman like you to death, you deserve better, baby. You do. My past makes me forever a part of this life."

"But why Danny! Why?" she cried out, "Don't you love me?" She trembled.

"Yes, I love you. You know that."

Monica got down on her knees, pulling Danny close, laying her face on his midsection, crying. "So give this pill-selling life up for us!"

Dropping his head he figured he might as well tell her the truth or at least another part of it.

"I didn't give you the entire story. I'm wanted by the feds for some murders, maybe for some RICO case or CCE charges, a lawyer I talked with says it's over for me. Let's not make this harder on me, and just leave please."

Crushed, she jumped up, wrapping her tear-soaked body around him. "Please just tell me this is a cruel joke."

When she realized there would be no smile forthcoming she kissed him, sensing this might be her last time seeing him alive. "Make love to me, for the last time, please. Just make love to me," she begged, pulling off his clothes.

Even though Danny wanted the pain of parting ways to be over with, his body, heart and soul craved Monica one last time. Once they tore one another's clothing off he sat her on the loveseat and they kissed from head to toe, that's when Danny couldn't resist working his way back to her garden. Sucking on her pussy lips, and using a finger to please her clit, Monica gripped his head as her sensational juices overflowed all over his face.

Bending her over, Danny sucked on her center a little longer, enjoying her flavor and the sounds of her moaning and crying "Shit! Danny, eat my pussy, ahhhmmm!" Sucking up her cum, he spit it on her asshole and pushed his thumb in causing her to hiss. Spreading her cheeks some more, he dove the length of his dick deep into her honey pot, filling both holes, making her buck like an untamed bronco in a rodeo. "Throw that ass back!" he demanded, smacking on her booty cheeks. "Damn I love this good! Pussy," he yelled, his eyes squinted tight, now closed.

As Danny hammered more of his dick inside her she started praising him, "Fuck me baby! Fuck me! I love this dick! Don't take this dick away, shit fuck me harder, harder, kill this pussy!"

As he gripped her hips and really started drilling her with unforgettable back shots, she began gushing all over the loveseat. Her vaginal walls quivered and contracted. Danny, still slamming into her womb suddenly felt the tingle of an explosive orgasm surging up his nut sack "Shit! I'm cumming in you!" he moaned, buckling down beside her, relieved. At that moment the weight of his world wasn't on his shoulders anymore.

"I love you Danny."

Picking Monica up, carrying her into the bedroom, he laid her down and said, "I love you too."

Waking up at 4 in the morning, Danny was moving throughout the house like a burglar. He knew this was the only way to get away from Monica without her crying.

Loading his weaponry, a duffle bag full of cash, and Forbidden into the Charger, Danny hit the highway headed to where it all began. As he drove, watching the sun come up, he swallowed a couple double stacks, and took a swig of bottled water. He reflected about everyone who knew about him killing somebody. He had considered East St. Louis as St. Louis, even though technically it wasn't. His very first thoughts drifted to that little boy, and Sugar Man.

"But that was so long ago," he whispered.

The only people who could take the stand in court on that killing would be Alexis, Olivia and Uncle Harold. Ruling them all out, he was left with the bullshit with Chino and Becky...

The thought of Becky's screams for help made goose bumps appear, so Danny headed straight for her house. Seeing all the lights were out, he looked at his watch, it was going on 7:30. Under these conditions, he parked his Charger down the street. After grabbing Forbidden by his leash, and his loaded .45 he began walking back to Becky's. In order to keep his facial features a mystery to people leaving for work on this morning. He pulled his black hoodie low. After calling her phone back to back, Becky finally picked up.

"Hello," she whispered.

"Where you at?"

"Huh?"

"I said, where you at?"

"I'm ... at the hospital."

Shocked a bit by her answer, he began to recall the gunshot explosion he heard when they last talked. "Who did it? And are you okay?" he inquired, grinding his teeth. But in the back of his head he figured it was the folks.

"I'm in Intensive Care, I'll survive. I'm a tough girl. Where are you at?"

With a smirk he said, "I'm where you want me at."

"Oh really, so why don't I see you?"

"Because it's a lot going on, on both our ends, we need to talk," he said, pondering his troubles with the law.

"Yeah, we do. When can I see you?" she asked, in a drowsy way.

Not knowing who he could trust, he chose his words wisely and cautiously. "Just know I'm in the city, so heal up boo. You ain't got nothing to worry about."

*****

2 months later…

"Let me get 50 on pump 4," said Danny while passing the gas station cashier a hundred-dollar bill.

After being back in St. Louis for a few weeks Danny knew that staying there wasn't a good idea.

It was like everywhere he went he saw a black sedan, and all he could think about was the feds was on him. So with Forbidden, he left there and had been in Springfield, Illinois ever since, networking with serious dog men there. He was shocked that they even knew about the upcoming match between the infamous Tina Marie of Shut 'Em Down Kennels," and Ma-Ma of Ecstasy Kennels.When he told them he was the founder of Ecstasy Kennels, they laughed.

As he was pulling off, after pumping his gas, Becky was hitting his cellphone. They had developed somewhat of a relationship since he'd been on the run. She was faithfully supportive, Western Unioning him about a grand every couple of days. But he still had a question mark above her head. And for some reason Danny rested better after finding out Chino was dead, maybe because a dead man can't testify in court. "What's up bae?" he answered Becky's call.

"Nothing. On my way to the gym, just was thinking about you."

"Oh really."

"Yes, really. So when can I come visit you, because I'm missing you like crazy."

Thinking back to the last time he saw her, and the wild night they had made his soldier get hard.

"You know where I'm at, pull down B," he told her pulling is vehicle onto the front lawn. Even though he didn't know if Becky was the rat or not, Danny couldn't deny his feelings for her.

"Okay great! I've got a little business to wrap up, and later I'll be on my way," she stated in a happy tone.

"Alright. Aye, when you get here we need to have a convo about some things," explained Danny, not matching the happiness.

"Concerning what?"

"Us. Us, and the conduct we've been involving ourselves in."

"I'll call you when I'm on my way, okay."

"Aiight, be safe."

As Danny came through the front door, Forbidden was laying there in the foyer asleep on his back, his tongue hanging out. Chuckling, he remembered when Monica had called cussing him out about taking her dog. "Just look at it like this, I'ma always have a part of you, and since you got Ma-Ma, you're gone always have a part of me." He remembered telling her.

"Don't worry. I'ma always have a part of you in my life. I love you. Danny. Be safe," she said before hanging up.

Danny just gazed at Forbidden, thinking of Monica's match. The dog gaming blog said the stakes on this fight was to be well over 1.8 million dollars combined. Through phone conversations, with Monica, and video messaging, Danny could see Monica had

Ma-Ma ripped up like a Freddy Krueger victim. The upcoming match had been moved from Fort Wayne to Detroit in order to accommodate all the high rollers, the bigger, more accessible venue made it easier to fly in and fly out.

When Danny whistled, Forbidden jumped up, and became alert of his new surroundings. Looking down at Forbidden, he smiled. "Time to eat-eat?"

Forbidden barked, then shot to the kitchen.

While walking Forbidden around the seemingly rural area of Springfield, Illinois, Danny was noticing how the dudes were hugging the blocks. He knew they were trappin! But with the enormous amount of skittles he had, he wasn't seeking out nickel and dime hustlers. It was crazy how much you could learn from walking through an area, versus driving.The streets talk, and what Danny's senses were telling him about this street was these guys on the block were watch-outs and traffic directors. A guy sitting on the porch of a small shack called out, "I got three for twenty, joe."

"Oh yeah," said Danny as he tugged Forbidden's chain, "What you selling, weed?"

The guy had a blunt in his mouth, and walked closer, but froze in his tracks as Forbidden growled.

"Yeah, I got that loud pack." He grinned, blowing smoke out his mouth. His fitted cap was broke off to the left. The sparkle in Danny's chains caught his attention.

Danny pulled out a vial of pills of all color, he unscrewed the top and gave dude about 20 of them. "These is how you blow up

in this town, my nigga. Sample these and pass 'em out. I'll pull
back down on you later." Danny smirked. Then walked off.

"You ain't say what yo' name is joe?" asked the guy, still
looking at the pills.

"They call me D... D-Money."

"Okay, I'm Slim."

With Forbidden leading the way up the block, Danny could
feel Slim staring a hole in his back, and to him that was a good
thing. Because either he was going to get some money, or get
another body, but one way or the other Danny was going to wake
Springfield up.

Chapter 24

After being chased around St. Louis getting shot at, and actually hit, Becky started taking her security seriously. So now, everywhere she went, she made sure her body guards weren't too far away. She had been going to the gun range twice a week, and trying to gain full mobility of her right arm after a couple surgeries to repair nerve damage.

On this day, the whole time Becky worked out she was thinking of Danny. "If only you would just let me in!" she said to no one, flaunting her hips and thighs. She'd been working hard in the gym, she could see her reflection in the paint of her new black Hellcat Challenger. She loved her new vehicle. The glass and door panels being bulletproof gave her an added sense of security that any white girl selling drugs in the ghetto would need.

While in traffic, Becky called around to all her hand–to–hand pill pushers and told them to slow down distribution because it would be a week before she'd be able to replenish their supply. She looked forward to spending as much quality time with Danny as she could. You would have thought her near-death experience would have made her back peddle out the game; to the contrary, it inspired her to go harder.

195

Stopping off at a mom and pop's diner on the outskirts of the Lou, for a roast beef sandwich, Becky saw Uncle Harold inside, he was hunched over an empty plate, sitting beside a guy.

"Hey Harold." Becky smiled.

"Uhh, hey Becky. What's going on?" he asked, twiddling his thumbs, somewhat nervous.

"Oh nothing, just about to grab a bite to eat and visit my mom. What about you?" she asked, feeling a weird vibe. Harold even appeared to be sweating as he dropped his head.

"Oh, I'm just … uh, talking to my lawyer about, uh, opening up a new business."

"Okay, well you know if you ever need somebody to help with advertising, I'm your girl," she offered with a big smile.

Harold's lawyer didn't return the same good spirits, instead he seemed impatient as both his hands covered a manilla folder.

"Yeah, hold up," he said, standing up. "You know what? You can help me. You know where Danny's at?"

At the mentioning of Danny's name, Becky's inner radar went off. She'd become over-protective of her lover and friend. So when the white guy beside Harold looked at her, giving her the creeps, she said "Um, I don't know. I'm just his side booty, ya know."

"Damnit, well when you do get up with him, tell him I'm trying to get on."

"Yeah, I sure will. Good seeing you again. I gotta order this food I'm starved."

Sitting in a booth, she ordered her food, then texted one of her bodyguards for the day with "Get a couple pictures of them two dudes coming out."

After sending that text, the receiver of it came walking inside the diner with shoulder-length dreadlocks and a well-fitting tailored suit. His eyes were hidden behind Versace shades. He slid in the booth across from Becky.

Paying for her meal, almost too nauseous to eat at all, Becky was out the door and back on the road heading to Springfield. During the entire ride there, she had the craziest feeling and couldn't wait to tell Danny. Expectedly, after a Google Image Search, it came back that Uncle Harold's companion for lunch was a DEA Special Agent.

"What's Harold doing talking to the feds anyway? I sure hope he's not workin," she wondered out loud.

Becky cracked a smile pulling up to Danny's 2 acre hideout in the sticks. She was hoping he was adjusting to his new environment.

With her own key, getting inside the house, she found it awfully odd that it was pitch black. Danny must be asleep, she figured. Yet as she locked the door behind her she wondered about Forbidden's whereabouts. Turning around, she felt something brush against her lower leg, "Forbidden," she called.

Feeling around the walls for a light switch, Becky said "Baby, why you got it so dark in here?"

What she felt next, poking her in the back sent a chill down her spine.

"I thought you was going to call," said Danny in a cold-blooded whisper.

"I-I was but something came up, I forgot."

"Yeah, came up huh. Take yo' clothes off."

"Huh?" she said dumbfounded.

"Take yo' clothes off. Now!" demanded Danny, shoving the barrel of his gun into her back.

Out of fear, she did as told, trying to understand what was going on but she came up empty-headed.

"Is you working with the feds?" asked Danny sitting down on the sofa.

"What? Why would you think that of me?" she turned to face him, lowering her aching arms down.

Seeing him dressed in all black, aiming a pistol at her chest, she froze.

"So who all know about me killin' Chino's man then? Who you tell?"

"I didn't tell nobody. Why the hell you pointing that gun at me!" she cried.

"Because if you lie to me one mo'time, I'm going to put some hot lead into yo' ass. Now, I'ma ask you one more time Becky, is you workin' with the feds!?"

"Are you fucking serious dude? You're acting really weird. If I wanted you locked up. You would beeee locked up! If you forgot, Mr. Paranoid, I'm your supplier." Becky put her hand on her hips.

"I can't believe that's how you feel, like I do any and everything for you, and…you think I'm a rat!"

Hurt wasn't the word; Becky was crushed! She believed what she and Danny had was special, but now she felt it wasn't shit. Dressing in her clothes, she felt so embarrassed. As she pulled her panties up, Danny embraced her, wrapping his arms around her waist. Just that slightness of affection from him caused tears to fall from her eyes.

"I'm sorry Becky, It's just, I'm trying to figure out who's telling on me." He frowned, being honest, still holding her.

Breaking free, she turned around and pushed him onto the sofa, causing Forbidden to bark and show his teeth at Becky. Danny pointed down the hallway and that sent the dog running that way."So you thought it was me! After everything. After all the love I so freely give you, and show you!" Now her tears were really flowing.

As he tried to wrap his arms back around her, she pounded his chest like an African drum. But that didn't stop Danny from pulling her chest to breast. She fought to get away because it felt so good being in his arms, and to think he could have thought so low of her was emotionally painful.

"I know baby. I'm sorry. Being out here in this slow ass town away from the action's fuckin' with my mental. I love the streets. Depending on a woman to support me's not my thing. I feel like I'm locked up, I'm used to the fast lane. But now, somebody's talkin' too much, and their pushing me further in a corner. I'm sorry baby. Please forgive me."

Feeling the emotion, the flames of passion in his kiss, Becky knew Danny was real about what he was saying. That's all it took for the fire she felt for him to ignite into an inferno again. Engaging in a heated battle of tongue kissing, she removed his shirt, as he picked his beauty up, and carried her into the bedroom. There, he sat her down, coming face to face with her pussy. "You see something that belongs to you?"

"Ain't no question," he replied, spreading her legs a little wider than they were.

"Well get it then. It's all yours."

Straddling Danny's shoulders, until she reached her second climax, after that, it was on!

After cleaning herself up, Becky sent Danny out to the car for her travel bag. Inside the bag she grabbed the ecstasy and weed, and gave it to Danny. "Let me ask you something," he asked while rolling up a couple grams in a fresh cigar.

"What's up baby?" she crawled up beside him.

"Why you treat me how you do? Like ever since we met, you was sweet on me."

Thinking about their little moment in the bathroom, they both laughed.

"Honestly, I just thought you was cute at first. But over time, dealing with you, I started loving you. And I treat the few people I love the best I can."She slow-kissed him, "Am I doing a good job loving you?"

"Yes. Absolutely. Do you really love me?"

She said, "I love you more than life, Danny."

As the words Danny told her sank in, completely, Becky was so thrilled and excited. After giving him more kisses, she said "Welcome to my family." But suddenly, the mentioning of the word 'family' brought Harold's face to mind.

"Oh, wait," she blurted, "I forgot to tell you I seen your Uncle on my way in. Oh my god!"

"What?" asked Danny. "Was his petty ass wanting another handout?" he asked puffing on the potent blunt, reading Becky's eyes.She had something to say.

"He was talking about he's trying to get on. Whatever he means by that."

"Nawl, he just trying to leech," stated Danny, higher that he'd been in a while. He wasn't ready to do a whole lot of talking, he wanted to feel the pleasure of her juicy wet walls.

"Hold on Danny. He was also talking to some older white dude and looking really nervous upon seeing me. And I got goosebumps as I spoke with him and his lawyer looked at me."

"What that got to do with what I'm trying to do with you?" asked Danny groping her wide tanned booty in his hands, sucking on her neck.

"Because it wasn't his freakin' lawyer, it was a cop."

"A cop! How you know?" asked Danny losing his erection.

I had my people investigate it on the spot," she remarked. Pulling up a photo of the agent on her cell phone. "This is him."

"That was today? Shit!" asked Danny feeling tightness in his chest.

"Yeah. Is everything okay?" asked Becky, never seeing the facial expression Danny was now showing her.

"Nawl. Hell nawl, everything ain't alright."

Chapter 25

It had been nearly a month since Alexis had dropped her load, and she had already scored a good job answering phones at the hospital. She was so happy, and felt blessed that her baby girl was healthy; to have a new job, and even happier that her aunt was willing to play nanny while she was at work.

The only thing that she felt was wrong with her life was Stephon who was steady hitting licks with his uncle.

Sprawling out across the bed after putting the baby to sleep, Alexis was enjoying her day off so far. All that was missing was Stephon. He had left home last night and hadn't called or returned yet.

Alexis began sending Stephon a text saying: "Good Morning. Wish I could have woke up to you.#LAME" She threw her phone on the bed but it started vibrating like he was already sending her a 'Good Morning' text back. Instead, it was a text from LA. She shook her head, opening the text.

"Good Morning, hope you sleeping good."

With and unexpected giggle, she smiled. His corny lines, and his wholehearted kindness was turning him in to a good guy-friend.

She typed in "Morning, and I was until Butter-Butt woke me up."

Rolling out of bed, she decided to just sit up and chill, instead of going back to sleep. She could hear birds happily chirping outside her window, so she raised it up an inch, filling the bedroom with fresh morning air. Running to the kitchen, Alexis grabbed some strawberries, a glass of orange juice, and a banana. While back in her bedroom her phone was ringing. Grabbing the TV remote, she flicked to 'The Real' and swiped open the text. "LOL Poor baby. Well a few of your kisses will put her to sleep."

With a grin, Alexis considered how LA would always insert a compliment into his comments. She loved that. It was cute. He never slowed down in his attempts of making her his woman. From gifts to flowers, he was laying his mack down heavy and consistently, none of which Stephon was doing anymore. Stephon wasn't even around much, and it was getting worse. "Oh really, well what you doing up this early?" she texted back while eating strawberries.

Hearing the front door open, then slam shut, Alexis figured it was Stephon. The load of worry she was holding in was finally released just then.

Every other day, Stephon came home speckled with blood, and a duffle bag full of blood-money. Alexis felt in her heart that one day, he wouldn't come home ever again.

One morning, she lashed out on Stephon so bad that she blacked out calling him "Danny."

"Danny? Who the fuck is..." he yanked her up, "Danny?"

"Huh?"

"Bitch, don't 'huh' me! Who is Danny!?" he spat, banging the back of her head against the wall.

Thinking back, and up until today, it was like he wasn't the same person. The demonic look in his eyes revealing the darker side, Alexis never seen, that was frightening to say the least. After detailing her past dealings with Danny, Stephon tried easing her mind by stating he, "don't kill kids." But the horrors reflected in his eyes said different.

When Stephon came into the room carrying a duffle bag, smiling, she knew he must have had a successful night away from home.

"What's up baby? Give papi kisses."

"Where you been?" she asked, still watching TV.

"Damn, no hey bae, I missed you?"

The way Alexis looked at him, then rolled her eyes, Stephon knew she wasn't in the mood for jokes or games. Finally dropping his heavy gym bag on the bed, Stephon gazed over at her ringing cell phone.

"Where you think I been? And who you texting this early in the morning while I'm out puttin' my life on line?"

"Don't worry about that! And if you was here with me, instead of doing what you do, I wouldn't be texting nobody. So like I said, where you been?"

Alexis was pissed that Stephon had the audacity to switch things around on her.

"Ma, see. That's why I be ready to slap the dog shit out of yo' ass! Bitch, you know exactly where I been, and I what I do," he roared.

Unzipping the bag, Stephon flipped it top side down, turning up his lip as stacks of money began pouring out. Seeing all that cash caused her eyes to spring damn near out her face. She had never seen this much money at one time since her drug-dealing days.

"Bae...Stephon where you get all this money from?" asked Alexis, mesmerized by the mountain of dead presidents laying at her feet.

"What's up with you this morning, asking all these dumb ass question? You know who I am, so just be happy I made it home with the bag," he stated making his way into the bathroom.

Still trapped in a trance from the sight of all the money, she'd blocked out his comment. But when he slammed the bathroom door that's when Alexis snapped out, "Bitch?" She ran toward the bathroom, "I've got yo' bitch!" swinging the door wide open; he was pulling his shirt over his head. Even though he heard her voice, he never saw the perfectly thrown right hook! Stumbling from the unexpected blow, he rushed out of his shirt so he wouldn't catch another.

"So what bitch is you fuckin' got you amped to disrespect me?"

"See that's ya fuckin' problem! You always worried 'bout some low self-esteem shit! Do it always have to be me fucking?" He snatched her up by the neck, pinning her up on the wall.

Coughing, barely able to talk, she didn't back down and said, "Yes it does. You ain't been fuckin' me or coming home!" Her feet dangled, "Let me go! You chokin' me!"

Wrapping her legs around his mid-section so the weight of her body wouldn't be hanging, he felt her bare bald mound of pussy against his abs. Grinning like the devil, he said "Since you so worried about who I'm fuckin' let me just show you who I'm fuckin'!" He unfastened his Gucci belt buckle. His pants fell down to the bathroom floor. Just the thought of how he was about to dog her pussy had his manhood harder than a cast iron pipe.

From the lack of vaginal penetration, Alexis was tight down there. So with the swift, rough stroke Stephon delivered made her yelp as the painful, pleasure-ride began. Pushing against his chest helped her none because he just continued pulling her into every stroke! "Fuck! Shit baby, damn. Owww! Oh my god!" she screamed.

Looking down at the point of penetration, Stephon was enjoying how her love liquids were dripping. "Damn this pussy wet and tight," he cooed. Slowing his stroke, he carried her to the bed, laying her there and continued to dick her down on top of all the money. He sat Alexis on an obtuse angle where she could see his dick sliding in and out of her, which turned her on even more. "Bae... babeee, I'm c-cum, mmmm, cumming!" she purred, literally drenching his cervix-deep pleasure tool. Pulling out of her is when he snaked completely out of his pants, giving her just enough time to sit up and suck all of her sweet juices off his dick. Tilting her head back, taking him deeper into her mouth is when he started humping her face. Alexis began to gag, he paused, and told her to "bend over!"

This was a dream come true for Alexis, to be getting the best sex ever on a bed of cash. She knew she was soaking the money with her wetness as the bills clung to her body. "You love dis pussy? You got me so wet! Damn! Ahhhhh!"

Pushing his thumb into her asshole caused Alexis to start bucking; her sugar walls were pulsating, causing Stephon to shoot off deep inside her womb. As he was now kissing the back of her neck, their daughter started crying. "Ow, watch out bae," she said, pushing him off. "That's Alexa, aw, mami and papi woke that baby up." She ran into the nursery.

Deciding to bring Alexa in the bedroom to see her daddy, and all the money he'd brought home; but when she saw Stephon going through her phone she smelled trouble. She about faced!

"Who the fuck is this dude?" asked Stephon, still reading their texts.

"Umm... that's LA, he... umm, a friend," she assured Stephon.

From the way he stood up and looked at her, she knew if Alexa wasn't in her arms he would have slapped her into the middle of next month.

"So you doing all this tripping with me and you the one with male friends."

"For one, it's not like that, and I be tripping because you be out fucking them hoes and don't be coming home."

"So what's it like, really because I'm dying to know?" He sat on the bed.

She knew this day was going to come, but on the inside, she prayed it didn't. Now here they were. Out of her peripheral vision she could see him tapping his feet, now, crossing his arms on his chest. He was getting impatient and was ready for some answers.

"He the dude I was telling you about when I said I probably had a lick for you."

"Then what? That was almost forever ago."

"Well, I found out some things, but we don't have to do that now you got all that money."

"Nah, you full of shit. What we gone do is hit that lick, and you're gone stop pillow talkin' to that lame," demanded Stephon, passing her the phone.

Looking from the phone to him, she was clueless of what was next. "What?" she shrugged her shoulders. "Why you lookin' at me like that?" she asked, kissing the baby.

"The fuck you mean what? Put that play in motion!" he commanded. Standing up, Stephon walked into the bathroom and turned on the shower. Hearing the running water, Alexis began holding her baby close to her heart.

Every night Alexis would pray Stephon would call it quits and get a job. But every day that never happened. And from the direction he was taking, that was never going to happen. So instead of doing as he told her to do, she waited for him to get out the shower, because she felt they needed to talk more.

Putting the baby in her crib, and turning on Sponge Bob, she dressed and waited for Stephon to come out the bathroom. When he finally did, he asked "Did you do that yet?"

"No I did not. We need to talk," she said, holding her ground.

"What you mean you didn't? See that's the fuckin' problem, you don't listen to shit I say."

"Stephon be honest with me, if I do this, is you going to stop robbing?"

The look in his eyes said he wasn't going to. Yet, he didn't want to lie, so why not dance around the question. "Why does it matter? This how I've been supporting me, you, and our family."

"Okay, and I understand that but when is enough, enough?"

"When I say it is! When my babies have any and everything their hearts desire."

"But you promised me. If I do this will you stop robbing?!" she asked stomping her foot.

"Alright, well set the lick up, and if it's worth it then I'll stop."

"Baby, how much money is this?" she asked, standing beside the bed.

"Shit, that's better than 500-grand," he replied with a grin filled with pride.

"And," she started with, choking at the thought of so much cash, "that's not enough for you to stop?"

He shook his head, "No."

"We have everything we need and want. A house, cars, clothes, jewelry, what else…what else you want?"

Stephon walked over to his daughter, picking her up. He gave her a kiss on the forehead, nose and cheek, causing her to laugh.

Alexis smiled.

"Ma, there will never be enough. As long as we have needs and wants. We going to always need money. The question is:

Why you pussy-footin' when it comes to setting this damn thang up? What… you got feelings for dude?"

"It's not that. I don't want to be bait. What if something happen and—"

Cutting her off, Stephon said, "Don't think like that. Aint shit gone happen. Not to either of us. And why would you even think I'd use you as bait?" asked Stephon, sitting his beautiful heart back in her crib.

Lost for words, Alexis didn't know really what to say, because the truth was, she was madly in love with Stephon. When she didn't reply to his question, he knew her feelings for dude were strong. Instead of blowing a head gasket, he sat down and called her to him.

After breaking it down, how it was going to go, Alexis felt a little better.

"So that's it? We going to just tie him up, ransack the house, and take whatever we get?"

"Right, just like that, ma," he agreed while wrapping his assuring arms around her, kissing her.

Purring as he caressed her body, she believed every word he expressed. She was more than ready now, to put in work with her future husband.

*****

Finding out that Uncle Harold was a rat was a crushing blow. Never in Danny's life did he think his very own flesh and blood would do him like this. Now he had to bring himself to murder the man he once looked at like a father, or go to prison for life.

211

With prison not being an option, Danny was laying in bed in the darkness, pondering on what the laws of nature required of him. It was about survival. Survival of the fittest. Danny knew that sexy women would bring the average man out of hiding. But not Uncle Harold. He would take a woman to a dog fight before taking her to bed. With that in mind, he felt the best place to catch Uncle Harold would be at the match up in Detroit. Looking at his Rolex, he figured he needed some rest before the long ride up to Detroit. With Becky asleep right beside him, Danny drifted off to sleep.

*****

It felt damn good to be back on the scene, but the order of the night wasn't pleasure, it was murder.

People were everywhere for this long-awaited event, people knew who Danny was, so he had to play it incognito. Having grown his beard out, and donning dark shades he moved like running water. From a distance he saw Monica beneath a gigantic red sign that read "Ecstasy Kennels." Seeing her did something to him. He missed her. So from a safe distance he observed his woman preparing Ma-Ma for the fight of her young life. Ma-Ma look dangerously sexy. As the dogs were weighed in, both were given baths to prevent any chemical agents from being rubbed on either dog. With this kind of money on the line and in the building, all precautions were taken.

Monica was shaking her father's hand when Danny noticed Uncle Harold enter the structure. He was carrying a kennel full of pit bull puppies, and they were in the kennel going at it. It didn't take long for him to sell them all either. With that money he'd made, Uncle Harold seemed to be placing bets and paying debts. Danny dialed Becky's number. She was out in the car observing things, from afar.

"You see him?" she answered.

"He's in my sight right now," explained Danny. "When you hear the cheering, you'll know the match started. Security will be more interested in the match, than you. That's when you bring the hammer inside and put that black wig on too."

"Ten-four," said Becky, screwing a six-inch silencer on the tip on Danny's Glock.

Danny rocked back and forth, thinking about childhood memories he and his uncle shared growing up. It's a shame it had to come to this, he thought. In the back of his mind he knew he loved Uncle Harold. So to keep him from suffering too much pain, he figured he'd shoot him in the head a few times. With Uncle Harold's muscle mass, he could probably eat a few bullets fired at his chest. Danny kept his eye on the big imposing man as he headed towards Monica. Monica threw up her hands after shaking his hand and went back to sweet- talking Ma-Ma. Seeing Monica bent over sent ripples of lust straight to Danny's manhood. It was killing him not to be out there beside her, and it was because of Harold he wasn't.

"Shit!" said Danny losing sight of Uncle Harold. Climbing down off the bleachers he looked all around for his mark. Harold was holding a conversation with a man who resembled the white guy in the photo Becky had shown him previously. The federal agent! Before Danny could spin around, the crowd started chanting "Tina! Tina! Tina!" And as calm as ever, Tina Marie sat in her

213

corner observing her opponent. She had nothing but murder on her mind tonight! Without haste, Danny made his way back to the car with Becky.

"Let's bounce! That same cop's in there. I saw Uncle Harold talking to him."

Becky pushed the ignition 'start' button then pulled into the darkness of Detroit's suburbs.

"Look up there," pointed Becky at the cluster of helicopters patrolling the night sky above, as she carefully maneuvered onto a main roadway. Just then, a fleet of dark-colored unmarked vehicles inched by.

Danny ducked down beneath the dashboard, "Shit!" he whispered.

"Stay down," said Becky, "they're going by us."

"Let's get on the highway, and abort this mission. I got outta there just in time. Shit!"

Becky kept her eyes in the rearview mirror and made a right hand turn.

Chapter 26

Her heart was beating like crazy when Alexis asked, "Stephon are you sure this will work?" "Yeah, I'm sure. This what I do, just trust me," he explained. "He won't even suspect you're involved," he added before getting in his new Lincoln truck.

The masterplan was for Alexis to go chill with LA like she had been doing. And for her to keep his attention while he broke in through a window.

Alexis was terrified that this was going to fail. She'd never played a role in anything such as this. Pulling off, she was still mad at Stephon because he promised her she wasn't going to be 'bait,' and as she analyzed the endeavor, that's exactly what she was. Her nerves were shot! But if this was what it took to keep the love of her life happy, then she would do it.

Perking up, she called LA, pushing her fears to the back of her mind.

"Where you at shorty?"

"I'm pulling up," she said, "right now."

"Bet. Well pull into the garage, I'm in the kitchen cooking." He hung up.

Just hearing his smooth deep voice, she was ready to back out. But she knew it was far too late, the wheels were in motion.

Once inside, he could obviously feel the change in her vibe, so he tried reading her body language. His eyes undressed her, removing the black leggings hugging her thighs. Her jet-black curls hung down her shoulders, giving her such an erotic look. But her eyes, they told a sad story. "What's wrong with you tonight baby? You look sick or something."

"Oh nothing, I'm just hungry and got a little headache," she said, massaging her temple.

"Yeah, well how about you go lay down for a minute till the food's done. There's some Bayer in the medicine cabinet in the bathroom."

With that, she walked into the bathroom, and took the pain-relieving tablets. While in the bathroom she unlocked the window. That's when she headed for the bedroom, unlocking the window as gently as she could. She laid there in bed after flicking on the TV. The 10 o'clock World News was on, but before she turned the channel, she looked and listened in. "In Detroit tonight, federal and state authorities arrested and charged 81 people in the nation's largest federal dog fighting conspiracy. In what was dubbed the match of the decade between two well-known rival dog gaming kennels, authorities conducted a raid in the middle of the night, netting 40 luxury and recreational vehicles, 96 guns, 83 fighting pit bull, and close to 1.9 million in cash. Operation 'Ecstasy' snared several men wanted by the FBI and ATF, as well as two Detroit Lions football players, however this man," Danny's photograph appeared, "Daniel Garcia is wanted in a string of violent homicides spanning from Detroit to St. Louis. Somehow – authorities say – he evaded capture. He is considered armed and dangerous. If you have any info..."

Alexis just laid there as if she seen a ghost. She flicked the TV off and went back into the living room. "LA, boy that room freezing and I'm starving. You ain't got nothing I can snack on?" She stood there rubbing the goosebumps on her arm.

"Ummm... yeah, it's some cherries in there and grapes," he said nodding to the refrigerator. "You said it's freezing in there? Was it a window open?" A look of suspicion engraved itself on his face.

"Umm. I'm not sure, why?" she asked sitting down at the table.

"Because I never leave windows open, stay here," he commanded, while making his way to the living room to arm himself. But that was cut short when LA and a ski-masked man locked eyes. "Oh shit!" he yelled, "Alexis, get down!" He turned rushing toward the couch, diving! Boom! Doom! Boom!

Hearing the thunder of the gunfire, Alexis threw herself to the floor. This is not how this was supposed to go down, she thought. Crawling on her hands and knees she saw LA was hit as his blood stained the carpet. He was reaching under the sofa cushion with one hand, his other hand trying to stop the out-pouring of blood by clutching his side. The masked man took point-blank aim, "Move again, and you and that bitch gone die together!" LA froze his hands where they could be seen.

Seeing Alexis made her way beside LA the robber said "Where that shit at?"

"What shit? Don't know what you talking about, ahhh."

"Oh so you think I'm playing? Tie him up!"

Doing as she was ordered, using his belt to restrain his arms behind his back, she cried. Sitting him up, Alexis saw the growing red puddle forming from the hole in his right side.

"Oh my god! LA, please don't die!" she begged.

"Shh. It's okay. I ain't gone die."

"Oh yes you is! Unless you're wise and tell me where that motherfuckin' money and work at. I'ma kill both yall!"

With that threat being issued, and real, it was time to either hold or fold. LA thought, feeling the pain. "Aiight, look, it's some keys on the kitchen counter to unlock the back room. The money under the mattress, and the bricks in the closet." Feeling the burning sting, LA grunted.

"Sweetheart, I'm gonna need you to get that key and open up that door."

Seeing Alexis zoning out, dude started snapping his fingers. "Hey! Do you hear me!?"

"Huh? Yes."

"Okay, get the key, open the door so I can get the fuck outta here."

When she keyed the door, pushing it open, a huge pit bull's head came out. Frightened, she shot into the other bedroom. "What the..."

This was becoming way too much for her. She was confused, and didn't know how this was to play out, but at this moment, she wanted out.

Boom! Boom! Boom!

Flinching once she heard the gun shots, she put her ear to the door. All she heard after that was noises like someone was moving furniture around. She ran to the bedroom window. It was open. "Please don't be dead, please don't be dead," she chanted running back to the door.

What tripped her out the most was she did not know who she was praying for. She peered out into the hallway to see the pit bull laying on its side with a hole in its head and chest. When she saw the dog's legs twitching she vomited.

Trembling, walking slowly into the living room, Alexis screamed, "Oh god no! What happened!?" Just like the dog, LA had a cavity in the side of his face. The gruesome sight of it all caused her legs to get weak. That's when everything went black!

When Alexis opened her eyes, she was in bed in nothing but one of Stephon's T-shirts. He was sitting at the edge of the bed holding their daughter, watching cartoons.

"Mmm... bae, why does my head hurt?" asked Alexis "Mmm. Feels like you hit me with a hammer?" Before he answered, she hoped everything was a dream.

"Cause you fell out and hit your head on the wall." With that clarification, Alexis knew it wasn't a dream. It was a nightmare.

"Is... LA... dead?"

"I see you really got some strong feelings for dude," he said mockingly.

"Is he?" she asked, revealing how bad she needed to know.

With a look over his shoulder at Alexis, he offered her a cold, soulless set of eyes, and said "yes."

From that day forward, Alexis felt her and Stephon withdrawing from each other. It wasn't that they wasn't in love because they were. Stephon's propensity for taking human life with no remorse was in conflict with her own morals. Both of them were willing to look beyond one another's flaws. So with raw love holding them together, they dove head first in their own line of work. For a while it all seemed to work. They damn near forgot about LA, and Alexis wasn't tripping anymore about him being away from home. But her intuition had been bothering her lately. So she kept Stephon in her prayers while he ran the streets robbing anything and everything.

All was well until Alexis got that call she always feared she would get. The one telling her that he was locked up.

Feeling as if her heart just fell into a nest of butterflies in the bottom of her stomach, all she could ask him was "What happened?"

"I can't really talk about it over this fed phone. But just, just get in touch with my lawyer, and come see me this weekend."

"I... okay bae, I will. You need anything?" she asked, feeling her tears welling up in her eyes.

"Yeah, send me like $1,500 dollars, and I need you to let my uncle know I said 'no go.'"

"Okay, I'ma get on it right now, I'll call him while I send this money online."

"Thanks ma. I love you."

"I love you too papi. Be safe. Call back when you can."

As she hung up the phone, a tear that was hanging on, finally glided down her cheek. It was like she was feeling the same way she felt when she and Danny split ways. Lonely, but when she heard her baby crying, she knew that was not the case at all.

"Hey babygirl. How's mama Butter-Butt feeling huh?" Kissing her daughter while holding her close to her heart, Alexis knew she wasn't alone as she thought. She still had her daughter and her aunt.

Chapter 27

As rays of early morning sunlight began cascading through the narrow slits of her very expensive vertical blinds, Alexis was awakened by the buzzing noise coming from her digital alarm clock sitting on the nightstand beside her bed.

Once again she had fallen asleep still dressed in her work clothes. She managed to wrestle out from beneath a thick red and green Gucci comforter to put an end to the annoying chime, then she unclasped her Rolex with the diamond and white-gold bezel and set it on the nightstand next to a small framed photograph of her daughter.

After she removed her midnight-blue business suit and her pink lace panties, Alexis just sat there on the edge of her bed massaging her throbbing left arm, still completely drained from the previous night's work. Her arm had been bothering her for several weeks now, but when her cell phone began ringing she was able to block out the tingling sensation she felt. And before answering the call, she quickly opened the drawer in her nightstand and pulled out a tan-colored 7-inch silicone vibrating dildo, then she crawled back into bed with it in her hand and answered the phone. She immediately heard the familiar recording that she'd been expecting: "You have a prepaid call from an inmate at a federal correctional facility. Press '5' to accept the call or press '7' to block any calls of this nature —"

BEEP! She pressed '5' and a man's voice came bemoaning through the phone's headset. Then she wiped at her stunning almond-shaped brown eyes and grinned. Of course, she knew it was her future husband, Stephon.

"Sorry I'm late, ma. They just opening up my cage for the day. You been waiting for papi?"

Before she answered, Alexis removed her silk and lace bra. "Yes, but waiting for you, papi's, taking its toll on my health," she replied in a whisper. "I'm trying my best to be strong, but—"

Stephon cut in. "Don't talk like that! C'mon, mami, it's hard enough on me dealing with the shit I'm going through in this bitch...stressin' and shit. At leas' you're free, Lex. Now, you collect that twenty racks yesterday, right?"

"I'm sorry...yes, I collected it."

"Good, go blow five of that on something pretty for yourself. I'll let you know later where to Western Union the rest. Understand me?"

"Yes, and thank you."

"Papi takes good care of you, right? So, you just need to stay strong for us. Now look, ma. You know what time it is, open your legs...let's play for a few minutes."

Without responding, Alexis parted her butter pecan-colored thighs, then began sucking on the head of the toy while gently caressing and running circles around her light-brown stiffened nipples. In her mind she visualized her man on top of her. Her entire body trembled as she seductively moaned into the phone before guiding the vibrating toy between her inner thighs while Stephon's deep controlling voice led her along.

Alexis enjoyed his slight Spanish accent, and inhaled then arched her back at the same time the head of the toy reached her clit. This aroused her and allowed her thoughts and imagination to carry her back to a time and place before her lavish lifestyle came tumbling down on her, before her arrest and prison bit. Before it all. Her legs began vibrating as the dildo penetrated her. "Oh!" she moaned.

It took nearly ten minutes before she finally reached a powerful climax and was able to catch her breath. She set the soaked toy on the nightstand while Stephon kept on chanting, "Beat that pussy up!" Then came a moment of silence.

"When you comin' to visit, Lex? I need to see you bad," he asked of her. "I need to talk to you about something real serious."

"Let me catch my breath!" she cooed. But before she could mumble anything else, there was a loud crashing noise coming from the living room followed by the sounds of footsteps clamouring across the hardwood floors of her two-bedroom condo. Paralyzed with fear, her mouth dangled open at the sight of two men in black jumpsuits and wearing ski masks as they came barging into her bedroom.

When she saw the Desert Eagle aimed at her head, she dropped the phone and that's when two sharp blows to the head knocked her unconscious. The larger of the two men started securing her wrists and the sounds of the duct tape being ripped from the spool sent chills of fear down Stephon's back as he listened in. His screams fell upon deaf ears. Just then three more armed men who were speaking Spanish and some broken English entered the bedroom and began ransacking it.

"Lex! Lex! Alexis!" Stephon shouted into the phone just before his 15-minute call expired.

*****

Alexis didn't have a clue how long she had been in and out of consciousness. As she came to, she realized she had a pounding headache. It all felt like one bad nightmare, as her only glimpse of vision came from underneath a slit of opening between the duct tape beside her nose.

Wherever she was, there was no sound. Only pitch blackness, and the stomach-turning stench of urine.

She wiggled around, yet barely able to, as she rested her body, hog-tied and all on a small pissy twin-size mattress.

Alex could tell she had been sexually violated, the pain she felt in her vagina and anus were excruciating. I'm so thirsty. she thought.But for the next hour all she could think about was her baby, and all the positive changes she'd recently made in her life.

The duct tape was unmercifully tight. So much so that her arms had lost all sensation. Then suddenly came a beam of light, an open door. Now footsteps. Alexis could feel the negative energy of someone on the bed beside her, followed by a cold hand that slowly touched her private area.

With tape covering her mouth, she struggled to scream.

But it was all in vain. It didn't work. She didn't want to die. Not like this. Not tonight. Snot drained from her nostrils as she tried desperately to control the tempo of her breathing. God please! she yelled inside her head.

As the intruder's fingers grew more forceful in penetrating her, the man's voice finally said, "So you and your boyfriend have been enjoying my money, huh? He sadly mistaken if he thinks he's safe in jail."

That's when things began to partially make sense to Alexis. Stephon's robberies had finally caught up with him, and here she was, caught in the crossfire. Her fate was now in the hands of an unknown man who had just thrust himself inside her! For a second she blacked out again. Alexis hated that she was so wet, but maybe that was for the best. Blocking out from her mind what was happening to her, she moaned and trembled.

"It's good," the man whispered. "But it's not going to get me my million dollars back, now is it sweetheart?"

He knew Alexis couldn't reply, but just whispering to her eased the agony of such a huge financial loss.

With unabated thrusts, the man began to fuck Alexis harder. Deeper! Making sure she felt his pain was a must, as he gripped both his hands around her throat. He grunted as his entire length invaded her womb. Yet, he had other plans for her once he climaxed.

*****

Stephon was having a nervous breakdown as he rifled through his legal material, pulling out his paid lawyer's business card. Next he slung his stack of paperwork all across his bunk and ran downstairs to the jail phone mounted on the wall of the overcrowded dayroom. He punched in the number and waited, slammed the phone down, and tried again. Then again.

"Hello?" answered his lawyer.

"Yes! This is Stephon Perez. I've changed my mind. I'm willing to cooperate with the government. I got info on many unsolved murders. I know where my uncle is hiding out at too! When can you get down here to the detention center?"

"I'll make a call. We'll be there in say... an hour."

Stephon hung up, but didn't notice the three Puerto Rican men concealing knives following him back to his cell.

To be continued...

Available Now

By Donald Reynolds

Ecstasy II

Haunted By The Past

For survival's sake, Danny realizes he must abandon his booming Ecstasy pill operation in exchange for a more honest occupation. Yet the demons of the past prove that they never sleep, they haunt, they prey, and if allowed to, they destroy.

In Becky's eyes, Danny is Godsent, and with his unborn seed forming in her womb, there is nothing in the world she wouldn't do to keep him from the jaws of the prison system.

When old acquaintances appear, envy surfaces, and evil intent rears its ugly head, there is nothing left for a queen to do but checkmate the threat at all cost. But is murder too high of a cost to pay for love?

UNCAGED MINDS PUBLISHING PRESENTS

ECSTASY II

HAUNTED BY THE PAST

DONALD REYNOLDS

The Ops

After losing his father to a lengthy federal prison sentence, 14-year old Mannie Johnson and his older brother Que realize they're now the heirs of a lucrative drug empire.

Before claiming the throne, Mannie's first test comes as an unexpected stretch in juvenile detention, where he makes a few allies, and one bloodthirsty enemy along the way.

While doing his time, Que's waist-deep in the grimy streets of St. Louis, regulating, expanding, networking, holding things down, establishing rules, setting examples, and learning the hard way that: Everything that looks good, ain't good for you. As he's recovering from a near-fatal ambush, Mannie's released, and he's hungry to do it way bigger than his father ever dreamed of. Mannie's young, restless, fearless, with a set of street laws of his own that he lives by: If you're not with us, you're against us. Being against us, makes you: The OP's... Opposition Beware!

Operation Black Bones

To be a gangster like his uncle West is all Chili wants to be. At his age, fast money and promiscuous girls seems to be the definition of life. But having been sheltered by his grandmother, he knows nothing about the pain, suffering, and bloodshed that comes with the title. Living in the illusion of rap music and urban thralldom, he desires nothing more than to have his opportunity of becoming a real street legend....

But that honor, Chili learns, comes with a price no sum of money can afford. In his quest, Chili not only creates clear and present dangers for all those innocent around him, but he also stirs up those ghosts thought to be dead and gone...

His new dreams give life to old nightmares and leaves a trail of blood so long that those resting peacefully in their graves cry out for justice...

For the past never forgets.

Uncaged Minds
presents

OPERATION

BLACK B**8**NES

a novel by

BLACK MIGO

Ghetto Lust

Erotic Obsessions, Twisted Fantasies, Dark Desires, Bi-Sexual Love Affairs, Hot Steamy sex! Brace yourself as you get ready to experience: GHETTO LUST

UNCAGED
MINDS

Ghetto Lust

A COLLECTION OF SHORT URBAN **EROTIC** STORIES

BY DONALD REYNOLDS
AND OTHER AUTHORS OF URBAN FICTION

Ghetto Lust II

A Salacious Collection of Short Urban Erotic Stories

It's no secret, dwellers of the urban ghetto are of a dark subculture where love is a rarity. Within this underworld, love is conditional, and dominated by vice, betrayal and lust. Lust and even more lust...

This raw, hot-blooded compilation of urban erotica lulls you on an unforgettable joyride through the sinful pleasures, and sexual complexities often found, like treasures in the jungles of the ghetto. The place so many call hell, or home. While others call it Heaven. You decide...

Embrace Ghetto Lust, prepare yourself to be consumed by it...again!

UNCAGED
MINDS

A COLLECTION OF SHORT
URBAN EROTIC STORIES

Lust II

BY DONALD REYNOLDS
AND OTHER AUTHORS OF URBAN FICTION

Greed Lust & Vengeance

In the grimy slums of Charlotte, North Carolina, two reputed rival drug lords find themselves obsessed with a beautiful, seductive and very pregnant exotic dancer named China, who's also a mistress of deception. Both men, armed and dangerous with extensive histories of violent criminal behavior, discover themselves virtual slaves to their uninhibited lust for the sheer pleasures China gives them. Slugs begin to fly when Raven seeks to unleash his jealous rage upon his sworn adversary, the passionate and charming fugitive Lamont King, for unsuspectingly moving in on his extremely profitable drug turf with a much higher quality of dope. Driven by greed and unable to obstruct Lamont's meteoric rise to power in the drug trade, Raven brings in the help of his gangbangin' cousin and his crew from Memphis's notorious LeMoyne Garden housing projects to settle the score. Meanwhile, Lamont develops a close-knit bond with China's crack-addicted father Irvin, and during the blood-letting and struggle for power, money and China's heart, unexpected circumstances arise that land both Lamont and Irvin in one of the most dangerous and barbaric-like federal penitentiaries in the entire U.S. for an armed bank robbery that they didn't even commit. The direct appeals are timely filed, but will they make it out of prison? And if so, dead or alive? If alive, vengeance is definitely in order

Greed
Lust
&
Vengeance

A novel by Donald Reynolds

Greed Lust & Vengeance II

Plans are made to murder a federal judge and prosecutor after China's man, Lamont King, and her father, Irvin Rice, are shipped off to a deathly violent U.S. penitentiary to begin serving a lengthy sentence for armed bank robbery. Meanwhile, it's back to the brass-pole and hustling on stage for China. Her career as a stripper in Atlanta is cut short when China's greedy and lustful boyfriend, Diego—a Colombian drug cartel member and enormously successful importer of cocaine—decides he has much bigger and more profitable plans for her. When China suddenly flees in a desperate attempt to reconcile her past, the present and then her future, bodies from inside the prison and those spilling onto the streets are dispatched with swift a vengeance to the morgue. And who, if in fact anyone, can elude the deadly bullets or the acute blade of retribution when karma calls? Only time will tell…

UNCAGED MINDS PRESENTS

GREED LUST AND *Vengeance* II

A NOVEL BY DONALD REYNOLDS

Book Order

_____Greed Lust and Vengeance I _____ $14.99

_____Greed Lust and Vengeance II_____ $14.99

_____Ghetto Lust I _____ $14.99

_____Ghetto Lust II_____ $14.99

_____The Ops _____ $14.99

_____Operation Black Bones_____ $14.99

_____Ecstasy_____ $14.99

_____Ecstasy II _____ $14.99

Shipping

Standard Ground (5-7 days) - $2.09

Order Total:

_____

Mail Order to:

Uncaged Minds Publishing

P.O. Box 436

Green Bay, Wisconsin 54305

Uncagedmindspublishing.com

Please be sure to include shipping address

Name_____

Address_____

_____

Made in the USA
Middletown, DE
21 May 2021

39809230R00151